Southern Fury

A MAX PORTER PARANORMAL MYSTERY

Stuart Jaffe

Southern Fury is a work of fiction. Names, characters, places, and incidents either are the product of the author's imagination or are used fictitiously, and any resemblance to any persons, living or dead, business establishments, events, or locales is entirely coincidental.

SOUTHERN FURY

Copyright © 2019 by Stuart Jaffe
Cover art by Francesca Resta

ISBN 13: 978-1-7337308-1-5
ISBN 10: 1-7337308-1-8

First Edition: March, 2019

For Gabe
Who came up with the title

Also by Stuart Jaffe

For more information visit **www.stuartjaffe.com**

Southern Fury

Chapter 1

STAKEOUT. The word sounded exciting, conjuring images of cops in shadowy cars watching for the exact moment a terrible crime went down, but to Max Porter, reality had proved somewhat underwhelming. Rubbing his eyes, he readjusted in the driver's seat and tried to stay awake. He really wanted some of that movie magic which could zip the night sky ahead until the moment he waited for arrived. At least, he had a good vantage point.

Parked in the back corner of the La Quinta Inn, he could see the front entrance and the side with ease. Not far behind him, the late night traffic on Route 40 rumbled by. Not so bad anymore — during the day, it had become a gnarled mess and would continue to be so for the next few years until workers finished construction on the downtown highway update.

Max sighed. Even getting into the city had become a pain. Everything had become painful.

On cue, Marshall Drummond appeared in the passenger seat. His ghostly form maintained the look he had upon his death — the handsome 1940s detective that wore a trench coat, a Fedora, and a simple suit with a simpler tie. Clapping his hands together with one strong hit, Drummond said, "Oh, good. Doesn't look like I missed anything. I love a stakeout."

"I can't imagine these things have ever been fun."

"I didn't say they were fun. They are a long, tortuous pain in the rear, yet when you get results — those moments make up for all that you endure. So, who's the target? A ghost? Evil witch?"

"Cheating husband."

"Seriously?"

"This woman, Mrs. Berkley, came into the office and hired us. Said she got an address for this La Quinta, date and time, all from his phone."

"Wife snooping through her husband's stuff. Real trustworthy."

"I don't really care. She paid up front."

"Still ... adultery cases?"

Max paused as images of flames leaping into the sky flooded his memory. "Everything we had went up with that fire. Gotta make money somehow." He did not want to rehash all that he and Sandra had been going through, so he employed a tactic that always worked — getting Drummond to talk about himself. "Why weren't you here earlier, anyway? Out seeing Irene?"

"It's not like that," Drummond said with a twinkle in his eye that suggested it was exactly like that. "For one thing, she's not a ghost."

"She's a psychic — the real thing — so I imagine there's some way she can be there for you."

"You keep your imagination to yourself. It's really not like that." Flicking his hat, Drummond leaned closer. "Irene is another living person in my life who actually cares about me. I've got you and Sandra and that's it. Having one more, one that doesn't work with me all the time, one who sees me in a different light — well, I'm just saying it's not the same thing. I got Miss 1800s always on call in the Other if I'm looking for a good time. For that matter, I don't know how I would do such a thing with Irene. And I don't want to know."

Max chuckled. "Once a ladies man always a ladies man."

"I was never that kind of a man. One woman at a time

for me. And I certainly would never be cheating like the bum you're waiting on here. I never understood that."

"Couldn't tell you. Heck, even now, with our current living situation, Sandra and I have zero private time, but I'm not looking somewhere else. I mean the last time we had —"

"Don't get into those kinds of details. I never want to hear it."

"All I mean is that even though we haven't, I never have the stupid thought of *well, gee, since I can't have sex with my wife right now, I'll go bone some other woman.* It makes no sense. And it's not only the betrayal and pain you'd be causing by doing it, but life is chaotic enough — why would you want to add to that? I always thought that was one of the benefits about marriage — it helped bring some stability to the chaos. "

Drummond snapped his fingers. "That's what I get from Irene — stability."

A sleek sports car pulled into the parking lot. Max thought it was a Corvette, but he couldn't be sure. He had never been much of a car guy.

Straightening in his seat, he pulled out his camera and watched through the viewfinder. His heart started pounding and he gritted his teeth at the idea that he might be excited about this kind of a case. When the driver exited, Max released his held breath and slouched back. False alarm. Unless their client, Mrs. Berkley, had married a twenty-one-year-old.

"Relax," Drummond said with a snicker. "You got it easy. I once had to do a job like this at a brothel. Can you imagine the number of people coming in and out of that place? Chances of me finding a philandering husband was easy. Chances of me finding the right philandering husband was a whole other matter."

When Max did not respond, Drummond went on,

"Look, partner, it is clear that you are on edge. Now, I know I'm not usually open to this kind of thing, but if you need to talk, then, well, I suppose —"

Max couldn't help himself. He laughed. Long and hard.

Drummond nudged his hat back. "I'm trying to be nice here. You shouldn't be laughing."

"I know. I'm sorry." Max dabbed at his eyes. "Maybe Irene Beck is good for you after all. I appreciate what you're saying. I'll tell you this much — and I promise I won't go too long or get too mushy."

"That's appreciated."

"We need a place to live. It's really that simple. We lost everything when our house burned down and the insurance company is taking way too long to pay and nothing's right. New homes cost too much and old homes have too many ghosts. Sandra sees them all over the place when we do a walk-through. I've never been happier that you're the only ghost I can see until we started looking at those old houses. Plus, we need room for four, and I'd like to have a study."

"I'm sure it's not a lot of fun living at your mother's apartment, but it's not forever. Can't you hold out until you get the insurance money?"

"It won't be enough. We lost our clothes, our computers, our everything. The cost to replace it all — it's crazy. And I don't want us rushing into things and making a mistake. We've got to do things right, this time. I mean we're not broke, but I wouldn't be out here on a cheating spouse case if I didn't have to be."

Drummond brought his hat back down. "Speak of the devil."

Following the ghost's gaze, Max watched a woman step out of the side door. She wore a long cloak with a deep hood as if she headed out to the Carolina Renaissance Festival. Scurrying across the parking lot, she headed to a rather plain compact — a Ford Escort — and dug something from the passenger seat. With furtive glances around, she headed back toward the hotel, clutching an object close to her chest.

"That's got to be her," Drummond said.

"Where's the cheating husband? And I never saw that woman arrive here. I think she had a room already."

"Even better. It means this isn't just a one-time fling. Looks like they've got a regular room."

As the woman swiped her keycard to unlock the side door, the object she held came into view. A book. A book of spells.

With the clap of his hands, Drummond said, "Looks like we'll have some fun after all."

Chapter 2

As Max hustled across the parking lot, Drummond floated alongside. Every footfall on the pavement acted like an accelerating metronome dictating the pace of his heart. Max had to admit that Drummond was right — finally moving, finally getting results in the long stakeout, had miraculously erased the hours of discomfort spent in his car. Even if nothing came of it, if it all turned out to be a false lead, he did not care. At least, he was moving. And he knew better than to think nothing at all would come of it. The woman carried a book of spells. Probably a witch. Whenever a witch crossed his path, something always came of it.

When they reached the side entrance, Max said, "Mind getting the door?"

Drummond bowed. "It's what I live for."

"You're not alive."

"Making my point for me."

Drummond's pale, ghostly form slid through the glass door and onto the other side. He turned around and paused. Touching the corporeal world caused pain for a ghost, and Max could see Drummond bracing before shoving open the door.

The second Max heard the lock disengage, he yanked open the door to minimize Drummond's contact. As he stepped into the hotel, he said, "Thanks."

"No problem." Drummond flapped his hands, then blew on his palms.

The corridor stretched toward the lobby — boring tan

walls and a patterned carpet that evoked nothing more than its utilitarian purpose. The place was clean and quiet which was probably all that most people wanted. The hotel was five floors with about twenty or so rooms, plenty of places for a witch to hide.

With an encouraging nod, Max said, "You know what to do."

Drummond's face scrunched up as he shook his head. "Sure, just make the ghost go through the whole hotel room by room. No sweat off your brow. You don't have to do anything to earn it."

"Sorry, did I not say *please?*"

"First off, no, you didn't. Second, maybe you should learn to do some real detective work so that you can find this information without me. What if I wasn't here?"

In a harsh whisper, Max said, "I'd go to the lobby to talk to somebody at the desk up there. I would have to come up with a lie, but I've learned some good ones from you. I think I could handle it. The real question is why are you still here? You are my partner. You want to be a good partner and do your part?"

"Okay, okay. Just thought you should learn to rely on yourself a little."

Grumbling further, Drummond disappeared into the depths of the hotel. Leaning against the wall, Max settled in for another wait. One of the doors opened straight down the hall, and a boy stepped out dangling an ice bucket at his side. It thumped against the wall like a drum tom. Max guessed the boy to be nine or ten. A voice inside the room said something that stopped the boy, but Max could not discern the words. With an overenthusiastic nod, the boy spun away and sprinted down the hall — coming up short when he saw Max.

The boy stood frozen. His hand clutched the ice bucket

as if it were a life preserver. Walking fast and stiff, he pressed against the wall opposite Max as he slipped by. At the end of the hall, he disappeared into an alcove with vending and ice machines.

Max listened to ice being scooped up and plunked into the bucket. There was something playful in the sound as if the boy had returned to his gleeful self. Moments later, the boy appeared and re-enacted his walking wall slide. When he reached his room, he darted in, and as the door closed, Max heard loud giggles.

"I know how you feel," Max said to the empty hall.

Less than a minute later, Drummond slipped through the ceiling and lowered in front of Max. "I found her. Room 207."

"Good job." Max turned back and headed to the end of the hall. The elevators were in the lobby, but he did not want to draw the attention of anybody working up there. At the opposite end, he had noted a stairwell to the side entrance. He climbed up to the second floor and headed down the hall until he reached room 207.

As he approached, Max pulled out his Glock 9 mm. He did not embrace the idea of guns, but getting closer to achieving his Tae Kwon Do black belt had taught him that there are situations in which having a gun would protect him better than anything else. Most people did not have to worry about such things, of course. Most people would be shocked to find themselves in true need of any weapon. But in his line of work, it had become evident that life-threatening situations were a more common occurrence than he had once expected.

He had only begun regular training with the weapon, so he did not put much faith in his ability to hit a target. Hopefully, the threat would be enough.

"Care to tell me what I'm going to find in that room?"

Max whispered.

Drummond wrinkled his brow. "You'll find exactly what you think you'd find. A witch casting a spell."

"Nobody else? Just her?"

"I'd have told you if there was someone else to be concerned about. And put away that gun until you can hold it with enough confidence that I believe you know what you're doing."

Max agreed he probably did not appear too intimidating yet. Besides, the gun was not loaded. He wasn't crazy. Holstering the weapon, they reached room 207.

The door stood slightly ajar, kept open by the night lock poking out. Max considered the possibility that this woman was no witch at all. Rather, she could be the mistress he had been searching for. She may have come to the hotel early to set the room up for a rendezvous with Mrs. Berkley's husband. Perhaps she merely role-played the idea of a witch.

But if that were true, Drummond would not have suggested she was casting a spell. He would have recognized a playful albeit odd liaison for what it was.

Unless what waited behind that door was a little of both. The mistress and the witch. Max gently pushed on the door.

The room — a suite with a bedroom connected to a room with a television, couch, and desk — was empty.

"I swear she was just in here." Drummond circled the ceiling as if a bird's eye view might help him find the absent witch. The coffee table had been pushed against the wall and on the open floor, a casting circle had been drawn with a fine white powder.

Max said, "You think this is —"

The bathroom door whipped open, and a black clad figure with arms stretched overhead stormed out. Max had only enough time to think — *that's the witch*. The next thing he knew, he was on the floor curled into a ball.

The blinding flash and deafening crack came to him only as a fuzzy memory. The smell of wood embers surrounded him. As the ringing in his ears subsided, he attempted to open his eyes. His eyeballs throbbed as if he had stared at the sun for hours.

"Max? You okay?"

Squinting, Max saw Drummond hovering above him. "What happened?"

As he struggled into a sitting position and fought back nausea, his ghost partner said, "That was the witch version of a flash-bang grenade. Doesn't work on me, though. You need a nervous system for it to be effective."

"Lucky you. Did you follow her?"

"Just because it can't hurt me, doesn't mean it didn't distract me. The light was bright. And, frankly, I figured I better stay here and make sure you're alive."

With a deep breath, Max attempted to get to his feet. Halfway up, he decided a few more moments rest was in order. "Did you get anything? Did you see what she looked like?"

"She was wearing that big cloak, remember?"

Leaning his head back against the couch, Max closed his eyes and held his stomach with one hand. "You mind being a detective and look around this place? I'm doing my best not to disrupt the crime scene with my vomit."

"I've already looked. Just a normal hotel room except for the casting circle. Rather plain looking circle compared to other ones we've seen, but I suppose spells don't care about aesthetics. We do get one thing out of this, though. On the edge of the circle is an old piece of paper with a name typed up."

"Let me guess — Mrs. Berkley's husband, Rodney."

"Not even close. Does the name Wilburn Walker mean anything?"

Max opened his eyes. He looked straight at Drummond and said, "Not yet."

Chapter 3

DESPITE THE LATE HOUR, Max headed back to the office. His head buzzed with the image of a cloaked witch and the name Wilburn Walker. No way would he be able to sleep — especially in his mother's crowded apartment. Better to get started on research. Besides, he had asked Drummond to search for Walker's ghost in the Other which meant the office would be empty and quiet for several hours.

Parking on 6th Street, Max lingered on the deserted sidewalk. Winston-Salem had grown a lot in the years since they first moved to the city, and it often became a hub of activity for people — especially with events like the River Run Film Festival and the Bookmarks Book Festival. But on a mid-week night, the city became a quiet town with barely a hint of being one of the top five largest cities in the state. Max usually disliked that strange dichotomy. He wanted the area to pick an attitude — be a bustling city or be a snoozing town. Choose one and stick with it. However, standing on the sidewalk, feeling the cool night air around him, listening to the gentle silence of a city asleep — he embraced the stillness.

After all, he had just encountered a witch. That meant the odds were high that his world would become anything but still.

When he finally climbed the narrow stairs, trudged down the old hall, and unlocked the office door, he knew he had been right to take a moment. Inside, he heard Sandra muttering to herself as she stomped across the floor.

"Where have you been?" she asked as way of a greeting.

"Stakeout. Remember?"

She rushed over and hugged him tight. "Sorry."

They held each other long enough for her to release some of the stress in her muscles. At length, she pulled away, and Max offered a smile. He had always thought of her as beautiful, always knew she was intelligent, and always respected the gifts she brought to the team, but in recent months, he had gained a new appreciation for all that made her such a formidable woman. Her strong will and keen insights continued to serve them well — both with cases and with life. She was his anchor. At the moment, though, he could see that she needed him to take on the role of anchor for a bit. And he could think of only one thing that would disturb her this much.

"I take it you had another fight with my mother."

"I swear she's baiting me now. There is no way she can really be like that all the time."

He could hear all that tension flooding her system again. Sitting behind his desk, he said, "Tell me what happened."

"Laundry," she said, folding her arms and leaning against her desk.

"That doesn't really help. What about the laundry?"

"Apparently, I don't do it right. Apparently, the boys need to have their laundry done in her special way so that they are comfortable at school and will do better at learning. It's laundry, for crying out loud. It doesn't make a difference if I fold it left or right, doesn't matter if I put in one swish of detergent or two, doesn't mean a thing. As long as the clothes are clean. And that was just the start of it. She doesn't approve of the foods I give the boys, doesn't like the rules I have in place for them, doesn't like anything I do. If I said it was a sunny day outside, she'd comment that the rain would be coming any minute. I mean, I've always known that she doesn't like me, but this is getting insane."

Sandra heaved a long breath. Max tried to think of something calming to say, but they had been through this too many times since moving in with his mother. Mrs. Porter goaded Sandra. Sandra reacted hard. Sandra vented her anger at Max. All grew calm until the cycle repeated. Any time he tried to hasten the process, to find words that might ease Sandra, she usually accused him of taking his mother's side and her anger reignited.

"I couldn't take it anymore," she went on. "If I stayed in that house any longer, I would've said something, or worse done something, and none of us want that." She leaned over Max's desk. "But I'm telling you right now, we have got to get out of that place."

"We will move out as soon as we can."

"You've been saying that for months."

"I can't force the insurance company to act any quicker. I've called them, and I've complained. But they're dragging their feet, and we can't afford a lawyer to speed them up. Even if we could, we don't want to push them any harder than necessary. We have to hope they don't start investigating too close because we have no idea how we could explain any of the things they might find in the ashes of our house."

With her hands on her hips, Sandra said, "That's a load of crap. We weren't dead broke when the house went up in flames and we're not dead broke now."

"We don't have enough for a down payment on a house."

"Maybe not a luxury home, but we lived close enough to that once before and I don't need it again. Do you?"

"It doesn't have to be a mansion, but it still has to meet all of our needs. And we need a lot. If we're going to continue the whole guardianship process for the Sandwich

Boys, then we're going to have to show the state that they're not living in squalor."

"There's five of us living in your mother's one-bedroom apartment. I think we can do better than that. The boys once had their own apartment, for crying out loud. They gave that up to be with us. We have to do better for them."

"Don't start trying to use the boys as your excuse. It's my mother that's your problem."

"No kidding. And if you want to see her live through the end of the year, you better start listening to me."

All their years of marriage had taught Max how to read his wife's emotions. Despite her vigorous debate, he spotted her easing shoulders and the way her hands dropped to her sides. She was still angry, but he had a chance to get through the thick wall of her stress.

"Come here," he said, patting his lap.

The corners of her mouth rose involuntarily. She quickly shut it down to a firm line, but she also sauntered over and settled on Max's knee. Her arms went around his neck, and she leaned in to share a brief kiss.

Something hard pressed against his neck, and he knew it was that ruby ring Sandra had started wearing. She said she found it at the bottom of her jewelry box — just a small thing with a small gem. Max could not recall ever seeing it before, but he caught her gazing at it from time to time.

Pressing her forehead against his, Sandra said, "I know you don't like the situation any better than me. The way she goes around calling you Little Max."

"What is with that? She's never called me that my entire life and now suddenly she forces it in wherever she can."

"I don't know. But it irritates you every single time. I can see it. And that's just a tiny example. You know things are driving you nuts, too. So why do you keep dragging your feet?"

"I'm not saying that my mom is right. She's not. We can do the laundry however we want and create our family the way we think it should be done."

"But?"

Max pulled his head back so that he could see Sandra clearly. "I think that she's right about the core idea. That we should be thinking about these things — about how we do the small things as well as the big things. It's not just us anymore. We're responsible for PB and J. It's been a hard adjustment, and I think we're getting there. Figuring out where we're going to live, what kind of house, what area, it's going to be the foundation of the life we create for those boys. It's that important. I think we need to take our time and do it right."

"And you think having all the money we can get from our insurance is going to make that much a difference?"

"I think we need to make sure these boys have a stable living situation. If we go buy an inferior house, then in another year or so we'll either be miserable or probably end up moving again. I don't want to do that to those boys. PB and J lived on the streets and lived in a ratty place of their own and they deserve to have a chance at a real home."

Sandra hugged Max tighter. "I agree." She kissed him before walking over to her desk. "There's no reason we can't be looking right now. If anything, it'll help the boys know that our current living situation is temporary. It'll show them and your mom that we are trying to improve our lives, trying to build a sturdy foundation for our family. And if you think waiting for the money so that we have the best possible options is important, then okay. While we wait, I'm sure we can come up with a rough estimate of how much were going to get and start searching now within that price range."

"As long as we're approaching it from the same side,

then that works for me."

Finally, Max saw a genuine smile lift on his wife's lips. "Then let's go back to your mom's place, get some rest, and in the morning, we can start looking at houses again."

Max tried to hide his frown. He quickly replayed the conversation in his head, attempting to find where the whole thing had flipped around so that he agreed to help her search for homes tomorrow. Though he trusted his wife to never use magic against him, she had been studying the ways of witchcraft for a long time. He couldn't keep his brain from raising the possibility that she had manipulated him with some other-worldly assistance. Of course, he dismissed the idea immediately. If for no other reason, he knew Sandra needed no assistance. She was smart — just a fact.

Besides, she was right. If he wanted to build the strongest foundation for their family, then he had to get out and search for it. Waiting to cross some arbitrary line only postponed the inevitable.

"Something the matter?" she asked.

With the evening's tension finally dissipating, he had no plan to shake the ground again. Instead, he jumped on the first thing to come to mind. "There have been some developments in our case."

"The cheating spouse?"

"Cheating with a witch."

"Really?" Sandra's eyes widened, but Max could not tell if she felt surprise or interest.

He told her everything that had happened that night. From the long stakeout, to the visit from Drummond, to the cloaked woman skulking around the parking lot, to entering the hotel room and finding the casting circle. He recounted the attack and finally revealed the name Wilburn Walker. When he finished, he saw the answer on her face

— she was intrigued.

"Describe the circle again," she said.

"Not much to describe. It was a plain circle made from a powdery white substance. Looked too thick to be salt. Maybe chalk. There was one symbol on the edge — a circle with a crosshatch inside. And that paper with the name was in the circle. I'm guessing we interrupted her before she could actually draw any other symbols."

"Maybe."

"What else could it be? I've never come across a casting circle that was mostly blank. You?"

Thinking as she spoke, Sandra said, "Meditation circles or other kinds of focusing methods might look like that. Not a casting circle, though."

"So, what's the matter?"

"That piece of paper with the name on it. That's the oddity. If she were doing a summoning spell or a curse or any serious magic, she would have completed all of the casting circle before laying the name down. If you had found a half-completed set of symbols, that would've made more sense with the idea that you had interrupted her. But this — it's wrong."

"Maybe she's a novice."

"Maybe."

Getting up from his desk, Max said, "Well, we're not going to solve it tonight. We've got a meeting set for tomorrow morning with Mrs. Berkley, and we can report everything that's happened. See what she says. If she chooses not to believe in witches or thinks we're crazy or whatever, the case is over and we don't have to worry about. If she wants us to keep going, then we're no longer doing a simple cheating spouse case and that means our costs go up."

Sandra snickered. "Somebody's been learning a bit about

business."

"Call it hazard pay. I don't care. But if we're going to be finding a new place to live sooner rather than later, then we could use all the money we can get." Max picked up his coat and headed for the door. He put his arm out for Sandra to link and as she walked over, he said, "I've got a good feeling about this one."

Sandra paused mid-step. "You just had to say that."

Chapter 4

AFTER A LONG NIGHT of being on stakeout followed by deliberating through a bump on the road of marital bliss, Max wanted to sleep an extra hour before heading out to work. But he no longer had that option. The Sandwich Boys needed to eat breakfast and to get ready for school. Since Mrs. Porter homeschooled PB, he needed to bring his books out to the work table in the corner of the living room. J went to public school, so he needed a lunch packed, and Max also had to get himself together for a full day of research.

He had two pans on the stove — one with scrambled eggs, the other sizzling bacon. He pulled out two glasses and filled one with milk and the other with orange juice. J stumbled in first.

"Morning, kid," Max said, forcing a light, joyful tone.

"Morning." J grabbed the milk and downed half of it, leaving behind a stark white mustache against his dark skin. "Hey, can I get some waffles?"

"Sure. Tomorrow. Today, it's scrambled eggs and bacon." He handed J a plate of food.

PB popped into the kitchen, his mouth moving loud and fast. "Sounds good to me. I'll have his, if he don't want it."

"Shut up. I want my breakfast." J shoved PB in a playful manner — mostly.

Wearing a robe with a floral print that may never have looked new, Mrs. Porter followed the boys. "See that?" she said to Max. "All your talking back is going to bite you."

Max stood by the stove, spatula in hand. "Who was

talking back?"

"You are. Right now. If all they see is you showing your mother disrespect, then that is all they'll learn. Children are masters of imitation."

PB smirked. "That's right. We're masters of imitation."

J laughed as he shoved eggs into his mouth. Max kept an eye on both boys for a moment longer. PB often instigated trouble. Max thought it mostly came from insecurity — both boys knew that J was the smarter one. PB had a few years of growth on J, but that wouldn't matter for much longer.

Mrs. Porter peeked at the stove. "Oh, Little Max, you be careful with those eggs. They cook quicker than you think. You have to watch things like that when you're a parent."

Sandra entered and both boys tossed out a boisterous *Good morning.* She rubbed her head as she pleaded with Max. "Coffee."

"Really," Mrs. Porter said. "Can't you see he's busy taking care of your children? I'll get the coffee."

"No need," Sandra said, her low growl baring more than simple morning grumpiness. "I wouldn't want you to go to any effort."

"No effort at all. If you pay attention, you might learn something. A good mother always knows how to anticipate the needs of those around her." Mrs. Porter filled a mug with coffee and handed it over. "Even for something as small, but important, as a morning cup."

Both women smiled with venom.

Before he could intervene, Max heard PB taunting J — repeating the same word over and over. *Nerd, nerd, nerd.* It had started over the last few days, and Max dismissed it as PB's jealousy of J's academic success. But he could see on J's face that the attack bit deep.

"Knock it off." Max pointed his spatula at PB. "There's

nothing wrong with being smart, and if I hear you teasing J again, we can quite easily end the homeschooling and send you to public school with him."

"Aw, I'm just poking fun."

"Does your brother look like he's having fun?"

J said, "We're not brothers."

Mrs. Porter pushed Max aside, swiped the spatula from his hand, and finished the eggs before they burned. "This is exactly what I'm talking about. Because you and your wife are not doing your jobs as their guardians, these two boys don't even see each other as friends anymore — let alone brothers. That's because you two are not building a strong family. I understand how hard it is, but I raised you and you turned out pretty good. I have the experience you both lack. I should think you would listen to me more."

Sandra set her coffee down hard, sloshing some over the rim. "It's not his fault. And it's not mine. And it's not the boys, either. They're a bit stir crazy, that's all. They've been like brothers since the day they first met on the streets, and even if they didn't both come from the same mother — let alone me — we all care about each other, and we all look out for each other." She turned her firm glare at the boys. "Isn't that right?"

The boys nodded without a sound.

Mrs. Porter said, "Now you're going to bully them into agreeing with you? I suppose you'll bully them into behaving, too. Wonderful parenting."

"Everyone, be quiet." Max's loud voice echoed in the silence that followed. He had not expected that to work and paused while he formulated something more to say. Like the captain of a naval vessel, he issued his orders. "Sandra, go warm up the car so that we can take J to school. PB, take your plate and go to your work table. Get started on your schoolwork. My mom will be with you in a moment. J, finish those last bites and get ready for school. When I'm done here, you better be in the car with Sandra. Mom, put my breakfast in a container of some kind and I'll take it to work."

Nobody moved. They all stared at him as if he was a crazy man wearing a straitjacket and doing a jig. Max slammed his hands together in one loud clap which snapped everybody back to the moment. The boys dispersed quickly and Sandra sauntered off as well.

Max stared at his mother as she locked her focus into finishing his eggs. Though she refused to look at him, he knew she listened. "You don't have to be so hard on her."

"I've tried to be nice," Mrs. Porter said, bustling about the kitchen yet never making eye contact. "I've extended the olive branch numerous times. She's simply decided to hate me."

"You know that's not true. And you know you're partly to blame."

Mrs. Porter jutted her chin at Max, and though he stood nearly a foot over her, she could still make him feel small. "I brought you all into my home. I moved down here to help you, for Pete's sake. I have done nothing but take care of these boys while you try to figure out how to become parents."

"And we have thanked you many times. We are not the incapable people who rushed into becoming guardians that we were. We are ready for the responsibility, so you have got to let go of some of it. I may not make breakfast the same way you do, and I may not handle the fights between the boys the same way you would, but I will handle them. Breakfast does get made. Isn't that really what all parents do? The best that they can?"

As if somebody had changed the channel on the Mrs. Porter show, Max watched his mother's demeanor instantly flip. Her face brightened, her body loosened, and she stepped closer with an overly-pleasant smile. "Oh Little Max, my sweet boy, you are right. You and Sandra have to learn how to be parents on your own. It's the way we all have to do it. People write books on the subject, but the truth is that the only way to learn to be a good parent is through trial-and-error. And the same goes for me, too. I have to learn how to stop being a parent and start being a grandma now. All on my own."

"Thank you," Max said, the weariness in his voice unmistakable.

"Clearly, this living arrangement is far from ideal. But I think it's gone beyond a little cabin fever. It's obvious now that the ease of being under my roof is holding you back."

Max shut down the flooding comments in his head about the *ease* of living under his mother's roof.

She put her hand on his arm. "I think it's time you move out."

Chapter 5

AFTER DROPPING J OFF AT SCHOOL, Max and Sandra drove to their office. Max wanted to share what his mother had said, but under the circumstances, he thought it wiser to remain silent for now. Once Sandra had cooled off from the morning's agitation, he would let her know that for once, his mother and his wife were on the same page. He knew that the fact that both women wanted the same thing — for them to move out — would mean little. Sandra had been burned by his mother too many times. For a while, it seemed like they might bridge the turbulent waters between them, but that had evaporated once they were forced to live together.

In the office, Max set about brewing coffee. There could never be enough. Sandra dropped to her chair and fired up the computer. As Max crossed the large, circular area rug, he paused.

He pulled back the rug. Underneath, a casting circle had been carved into the floor for Sandra's use. Though not truly a witch, Sandra had spent a lot of time studying their ways. Max never could be completely onboard with her decision to deepen her knowledge of witchcraft, but neither could he deny its usefulness.

He looked at the circle closely. Sandra was right. The circle in the hotel looked nothing like this. It had been nothing more than a circle with one lone symbol drawn in, whereas this one had concentric circles for different levels of symbols and spells. Whenever Sandra used it, she often filled it up with arcane writing and ancient glyphs.

"Better put the rug back," Sandra said, her voice hinting at the woman he knew and loved. He glanced over at her and she tapped her ruby ring against the desk before pointing at the door. "Our client will be here shortly."

Max returned the rug to its proper position before getting to work. By the time Mrs. Berkley arrived, he had put together two reports of his findings. One a sanitized version, omitting the supernatural elements, and another that bore witness to the truth of events.

When Mrs. Berkley entered, Max wished Drummond had been there. The woman looked as if she had stepped out of a 1940s mystery film — wearing a long coat with a wide belt and the collar up, a stylish hat brought down, and sunglasses. Her attempt to be inconspicuous and unrecognizable had created a spotlight right upon her. Taking off the hat and sunglasses revealed a Japanese woman with sharp cheekbones and thin lips. Long, black hair had been tied back tight, yet the tail still fell to the middle of her back. The combination of a traditional Japanese appearance mixed with an old American style created a strong, slightly intimidating quality. It set Max off-kilter, and if not for Sandra, he would have sat there staring at their client for far too long.

"Welcome, Mrs. Berkley," Sandra said, gesturing to a chair. "Would you like some coffee?"

"I'll go to Starbucks if I want coffee. I came here for an update on my case. I need investigators, not baristas."

Walking over to the coffee maker, Sandra poured herself a mug. Behind Mrs. Berkley, she made a face that forced Max to cover his mouth for fear of breaking out into laughter.

"Well?" Mrs. Berkley said, pulling out her phone and tapping away quickly.

Max cleared his throat and placed a hand atop each of

his reports. "I spent last night on stakeout at the hotel you informed us about. Your husband never showed."

"Is that supposed to relieve me?"

"We're not here to relieve you or worry you. Merely acquire the information you seek. The thing is that while I never saw your husband, I did find a woman."

"Oh?"

Sandra returned with a mug of coffee for Max. She made a point of handing it over before taking her seat. "Are you a religious woman?"

Mrs. Berkley's head snapped towards Sandra. "What business is that of yours?"

"This woman that Max encountered belongs to an unusual religion."

"Are you trying to tell me my husband's involved with a cult?"

Max picked up the sanitized version of his report and straightened the pages. "We can't be sure this woman is the mistress you're worried about, but I find the odds that we would accidently bump into a woman of her religion while on stakeout for your husband to be slim."

Mrs. Berkley set her phone back in her purse. She sat wooden — only her eyes gave away that she mulled over anything. But he couldn't even be sure she mulled over his words or something entirely unrelated to their meeting. "What kind of religion is this?" she finally asked.

Sandra said, "A pagan religion."

Mrs. Berkley's eyebrows lifted, and Max noted how large the woman's forehead was — her eyebrows seemed to float high on endless skin. She said, "You're talking about witchcraft. You ran into a witch?"

"You know about witches?"

"I pay attention to the important people — the Hanes family, the Reynolds family, and for a time, the Hull family.

You may not know that last one. They kept very quiet, but rumors abound of the darker things they were involved with. A few years ago, they dropped off the social landscape. Probably lost all their money to one witch or another."

"We've heard a thing or two about that."

Max set the stack of papers down and picked up the other pile. "Well, this makes things easier. Yes, we found a witch. And if you understand anything about witches, anything beyond rumors, you'll know that your husband is in serious trouble. These are not the kinds of people he should be messing around with. Forgive the expression."

"If he's cheating on me with a witch, then he deserves all he has coming to him."

Sipping his coffee, Max said, "Does the name Wilburn Walker mean anything to you?"

"Never heard of the man. How is he involved?"

"We're not sure yet. But here's the thing — this case has taken a different turn then the kind of case we signed up for."

Mrs. Berkley clutched her purse. "I thought this was exactly the kind of case you people investigated."

"That's true. However, you did not hire us to go after a witch. You hired us to get compromising photos of your husband. Now, we'll be happy to investigate this witch, to make sure her involvement with your husband does not compromise you or endanger you, but that will require extensive research."

"I see." She opened her purse and pulled out a checkbook. "I very much want you to continue with this investigation. Will one thousand for the week cover the extra expenses?"

Max worked hard not to choke on his coffee. "That would be sufficient." From the corner of his eye he could see Sandra's shock.

After handing over the check, Mrs. Berkley stood and went about putting on her 1940s costume. "I trust that you'll contact me when you have further developments. If not before, I expect to hear from you by the end of the week. Anything else?"

Max offered his hand. "I think that covers everything."

She glanced at his hand like it had some bizarre mutation growing from the fingers. As her footsteps receded in the hall, Max realized he had forgotten to give her the report.

Sandra approached him and squeezed his shoulders. "That went well."

"It's about time we have a win."

Picking up the check, she said, "This will definitely help with our down payment." She kissed his cheek. "Ready to go look at houses?"

Before he could answer, Drummond swooped into the room. "You guys are not going to believe this."

"We have news of her own," Max said.

"Great. Wonderful. Tell me your news some other time. For now, shut up and listen."

With less enthusiasm, Sandra said, "What is it?"

Max said, "I know — you found Wilburn Walker."

"Not at all. He's nowhere in the Other. But the news going around fast is far more important. Two members of the Mobley coven are dead. They were hanged."

Chapter 6

MAX HAD BEEN IN THE MOBLEY HOUSE on several occasions and it never got easier. From the outside, the house blended in with all the other suburban homes lining a quiet development. A few joggers ran by and a woman walked her dog. All very normal. But, of course, inside the house was a different matter. A witch coven lived there.

Max had spent a few times in their living room where they often entertained guests. He had been upstairs twice — once invited, once not. But this visit marked his first time in their kitchen. He found it no less nerve-wracking than any previous occasion.

Had he been sitting in their kitchen on less important business, he would have been nervous, too. Then again, he would never have come to this place on less important business. But when somebody murders two members of this witch coven, the most powerful coven in the Carolinas, paying respects could not be ignored.

Lena Mobley, a middle-aged woman dressed in a suburban façade that matched the house, finished preparing a tray of cheese and crackers at the marble counter. Despite her motherly appearance, Max knew better. After Grandma Mobley, Lena Mobley was the most powerful witch in the entire coven. Grandma Mobley had formed the coven over a hundred years ago, but Lena ran the day-to-day operations, and she would inherit the leadership when Grandma Mobley passed away — if that old witch could ever die.

The worst thing about the current situation — besides

the loss of life — rested in the fact that Max knew of only one group both strong enough and bold enough for such an attack — the Magi. Run by Grandma Mobley's rival, Mother Hope, the Magi gave lip service to the idea that they sought to protect the world from witches. Perhaps that had been true at one time. But under the control of Mother Hope, the Magi had become every bit as power-hungry and devious as the witches they fought against.

Max rubbed the spot on his chest where Mother Hope had cursed him. She used the threat of enacting the curse to control him. At any moment, practically with a snap of a finger, she could throw Max into a coma and leave him as a half-ghost, lost, neither living nor dead. The only defense he had managed against this curse was to link it to Mother Hope's right hand man, Leon Moore. But fighting fire with fire did not sit well — not when the fire was witchcraft.

Lena turned around and set the snack tray on the kitchen table. "I apologize for having to meet with you in here. We obviously prefer our sitting room, but under the circumstances, we need that space for other purposes."

Other purposes. Had he been eating one of the offered crackers, Max would have choked. The two dead women lay on tables in the living room turned parlor, and he knew that elsewhere in the house, Mobley witches worked hard to establish spells that would find the killers and exact revenge. Not that anybody had to guess hard where to look.

As Max picked up a cracker, he heard Drummond's gritty voice from down the hall. "Keep her busy. I'm checking out the dead women."

Before Max could choke for real, Sandra leaned forward as if she might offer Lena a comforting hand but held back at the last moment. "We simply wanted to offer our condolences."

Despite Sandra's comforting tone, Max knew she

seethed underneath. They were supposed to be house hunting. They were supposed to be setting the building blocks of a better life. Instead, they were talking with a witch. This whole day had turned into a mess and they weren't even close to lunchtime. Worse, they both knew that any conversation with a witch had to be approached with wariness and care. Or else they might leave with far worse than a curse over their heads.

Drummond floated under the archway leading to the rest of the house. "I just want to go on the record saying that this is a bad idea. These witches don't care whether you show up or not. You are not part of the coven and, if anything, you've only ever brought trouble their way."

Max wanted to point out that the only reason he even knew any of the coven members was that, in the past, they had hired the Porter Agency to investigate their problems. But it would not help, and he did not need to make the Mobleys self-conscious that a ghost was listening in on their conversations.

"Having said my piece," Drummond went on, "I'll let you know that things look strange in there. Back in my day, I saw a lot of suicides — The Great Depression and all — and I can tell you for certain that those women were hanged after they died."

Lena Mobley lifted a teacup but immediately set it back down. "What is it that you want? I have a very busy day ahead dealing with these deaths."

Sandra said, "Besides paying our respects, we wanted to offer our help. We know you can't go to the police — they don't believe in witches, and if some do, that's probably worse for you. So if it will help, we can investigate for you."

Everything in Max's mind screeched the brakes, yet he still heard the crash and twist of metal as his thoughts smashed together. He and Sandra had never discussed this course of action, and hearing Drummond's partial report on it confirmed how bad an idea this could be, but he could not get into a fight in front of Lena Mobley. That would give the witch too much ammunition.

Before he could protest, though, Lena sat back and crossed her arms. "No," she said.

"Good," Drummond said. "Polite offer, considering she's a witch, but you're lucky she —"

Max reared as if flicked hard against the nose. "What do you mean *No?* We're the best investigators of the paranormal and the supernatural there are. Somebody's murdered two of your people and you don't want to investigate it?"

"I don't want *you* to investigate it. Your constant association with Mother Hope and the Magi creates an undesirable conflict of interests."

"Just because we're stuck having to work with them from time to time does not mean we are beholden to them."

"What are you doing?" Drummond said. "You don't actually want to work for her? The woman said *No.* Take it and let's get out of here. I didn't even get around to telling you that those dead women were marked. Understand? The witch we found casting a spell about that Walker fella — well, that circle with the crosshatch symbol is on both these dead women."

Max locked his attention on the floor. He did not want to give away any emotions that Lena might pounce on. Sandra, on the other hand, tapped her ruby ring on the kitchen table.

Lena's face darkened. "Ugly things are coming our way."

"She's got that right," Drummond said.

"Grandma Mobley has been warning us for years that eventually Mother Hope's patience would end. Tensions between them have been bad lately, and she knew that this day would come soon enough. We would know when that moment arrived because we would start to die. And those deaths would be the opening salvos to a war."

"It doesn't have to be," Sandra said. "You don't have to tear each other apart."

Drummond drifted in, gesturing at Lena like a game show hostess. "Of course she does. Look at her. She's not going to simply sit here and let Mother Hope kill the rest of her coven. And a grim death, at that. You better believe Grandma Mobley's upstairs right now working on some horrible spell of the deepest and deadliest magic to retaliate. Please, listen to me. We should leave."

Lena stood and took her untouched teacup to the sink. As she washed it, she gazed out the window to the backyard. Max thought of all the neighbors. Nobody in the development would suspect that this simple house could actually be the seat of extreme power. It was like hiding dynamite in a bowling pin. Nobody would know it was there unless they tried to knock it down.

But now somebody — most likely, Mother Hope — was doing just that.

"The time is coming," Lena said. "Soon, you both will no longer be able to ride the middle. You will have to choose sides."

"Yes," Drummond said. "Choose my side. Every single time we come to this terrible house, I've warned you to leave and you both never listen. And every single time, I'm right. So, damnit, listen to me."

Max glanced at Drummond before answering. "Hate to disappoint you, but we're not taking any side. We're not witches, and we are certainly not interested in having either the Mobleys or the Magi take over control of our city or state."

Lena pressed two fingers against the corner of her eye and rubbed small circles. With a sigh, she said, "Grandma Mobley has been alive a long, long time. Just listening to her talk about the different decades she's experienced has taught me many things. More than anything, though, I've learned that in any conflict, nobody gets to play Switzerland. Even Switzerland never really got to play that role. You always have to take sides. And in this case — well, you should be careful. Things never end well for a man caught between two witches."

Drummond floated down between Lena and Max. "That's it. You offered your condolences and she's made her threats. Let the woman prepare for her funeral. If the two of you stay here any longer, I swear I'm gonna start sticking my hands in your heads and give you such brain freeze you won't be able to think clear for a week."

Sandra stood. "We thank you for your time. And again, sorry for your loss."

Lena nodded but her attention had drawn inward. She barely moved out of the way as Max led Sandra toward the hallway to leave. But Max stopped. He turned back and stared at Lena.

"One last thing — you ever hear of a man named Wilburn Walker?"

Lena gazed up as she shook her head. "Should I have?"

"It doesn't matter. Just wondering."

As they headed out the door and towards the car, Max made sure to keep his face away from view of the house. He assumed they were being watched, and he did not want any snooping witches to notice his expression. He couldn't hide his shock. Because no matter how much Lena might deny it, Max saw her flinch at the mention of Walker.

She knew the name.

Chapter 7

DRUMMOND FLOATED IN THE BACKSEAT as Max navigated his way through winding streets in an attempt to avoid the construction areas. The old ghost had his hat down, but Max could still spot the tight jaw. Less than five minutes into the drive, Sandra frowned. That small gesture warned Max that despite the clear skies and sunny weather, he headed into a dark storm. Heck, between his wife and his partner, he didn't like the weather report anywhere in the car.

"Hon," Sandra said in a deceptively calm tone. "You're going the wrong way. The realtor's office is all the way out on Miller Street."

Crap. "We're headed to our office. After everything we just heard at the Mobley house, it's clear to me that this case —"

"There's always going to be a case. It's what we do."

Max glanced in the rearview mirror. Drummond made a show of staring out the window. No help there.

"This is not just any case. The Magi are finally moving in on the Mobleys. You heard Lena — this is a witch war in the making."

"But that's not our case."

"You saw her face when I mentioned Wilburn Walker. I know you did. She knows that name. And if we've learned anything over the last few years, it's that all these witches know each other. They're all interconnected. The minute I saw a witch at that hotel, that was the point where our cheating husband case became something bigger. And now, with these hangings — this is not just an average case. This is serious."

"Every case is serious. But our lives have to keep moving forward. Life doesn't stop just because there are dangerous cases. There will always be something, and for us, it will always be big and most likely dangerous. Should we not have applied for guardianship of PB and J because our lives are dangerous? Should we just roll over for the Mobleys and the Magi because things get a bit hairy?"

"I didn't mean it like that, and you know it."

"Think of it this way — at the end of a long day, after dealing with witches and ghosts and all the dangers, would you rather return to your own space where we can hold each other in privacy and peace, or would you rather go back to your mother's apartment?"

"I'd rather not have to worry about that question until we stop the entire city from being destroyed by two angry groups of witches."

From the back seat, Max heard Drummond mutter under his breath. "You have something to say?" Max said.

Still focused outside, Drummond said, "I learned quickly that I should no longer get involved with your marital issues. Especially considering how uptight you both have been lately. When you're ready to deal with the case, let me know." With that, Drummond disappeared.

Sandra groaned and pressed back against the headrest. "Why is this so hard for you? I'm not trying to nag — you know I hate being that kind of a wife — but you seem insistent on making our lives miserable."

Max gestured toward the city. "There's a lot going on out there. A damn war is ready to blow up everything."

"Stop being dramatic. A war between witches is like a Mafia war. It's between them, and that's it. The city isn't going to crumble to its knees."

"You're only guessing. It's not like you've ever experienced this kind of thing before. Wait, have you?"

"Hon, you're losing it."

He felt hot around his neck. "This is just so nuts. I mean hanging those women. I guess I always thought a witch war would be dueling spells or something. But it's happening and I don't see what I can do to make it any better for us."

"For starters, you can stop pushing back on everything I suggest."

They had stopped at a traffic signal, and as the light changed to green, the car in front did not move immediately. Max honked his horn twice. The shrill cry of his car rang in his ears. Accelerating faster than necessary, Max's brain raced to find a solution.

When the idea formed, he thought it so obvious that he wanted to slap his forehead. "How about this? I'll stay at the office and do the research necessary for our case. You go to the realtor and check out the homes you're interested in. Narrow it down to three or four and set up appointments to check those out with me in the coming days. By then, we'll have a better handle on our witch that's a mistress and how it connects to the Mobleys. I realize that's not ideal, but at least this way, I can satisfy everybody's needs."

Sandra's mouth tightened into a small dot. "Fine."

When he parked near the office, Sandra got out, mumbled a goodbye, and headed for her car. Max did not pursue her — years of marriage had taught him when she needed space. Or perhaps that was an excuse, and he simply wanted to wait another day.

He felt the chill of Drummond's presence moments before he heard his partner. "How did you ever trick her into marrying you?"

Walking toward the office, Max said, "Thanks for the

vote of confidence."

"I really want to know. I'm no marriage expert, but it seems pretty obvious to me that she was giving you every opportunity to go look at houses with her. It's clear that it means a lot to her. Yet you screwed up the whole thing."

Max stopped on the sidewalk and stared at Drummond. "You were eavesdropping on us?"

A mother walking hand-in-hand with her toddler swiftly lifted the child and decided the other side of the street was where they had meant to be. Max took no offense. He understood that they only saw a man talking to himself in the middle of the sidewalk. He had to be careful about having conversations with Drummond outside. It would never help anybody if he got locked up in a mental hospital.

Walking faster, Max said, "Why doesn't anyone understand that there is a serious witch problem boiling over?"

"Because your wife and I understand the witch world better than you do. Yes, what happened to the Mobleys is bad, but this witch war has been brewing for nearly a century. It'll keep growing for a lot longer. Little explosions like this one happen from time to time. It's nothing to get bent out of shape over. At least, not in the way you're going about it."

"Then you're both wrong. Something different is definitely happening here. It's not chance that we got hired on a case that led to a witch and the name Wilburn Walker. Not when that same name pulled an unmistakable reaction from Lena Mobley."

"Okay, I agree with you that part of it is strange. And it deserves our attention, too."

A chill struck Max. Gazing through Drummond's pale figure, Max thought he saw a cloaked woman watching him. But when he side-stepped to see clearer, she was gone.

Drummond had not stopped talking. "Plus, you need to look up the symbol I saw carved in those witches' skin. The same one from the casting circle. And I didn't tell you the worst of it."

After a pause, Max said, "Are you going to?"

"I don't know. See, Sandra's right. All your hard work doesn't mean anything if you don't use it to live your life better and fuller. Trust me on this one. I lived a good life, and in my death, I watched generations grow up and grow old. I've seen too many people waste their lives away working hard for things that don't matter. You need to listen to her."

"You think what we do doesn't matter?"

"Of course, it does. But people have been battling ghosts and spells for centuries. Long before you were born, and they'll go on long after you die. You're not going to stop it forever. So, do your part, but don't let it ruin your life. Especially when you've got a great gal like Sandra."

As he entered the office, the bitter aroma of old coffee from that morning filled the air. Max looked over at his computer. "I can't change what I said. I'll figure out some way to fix that. But for now, I've got research to do. Because if you think Sandra's mad at me now, imagine how she'll feel if I don't turn up anything valuable after blowing her off for the day."

Drummond hovered in the middle of the room. He glanced at the computer and then at Max. "That's a sound point. For the sake of us all, I'm begging you, go find everything."

Chapter 8

DESPITE THE HORRID OPENING TO HIS DAY, Max found the second half to be pure delight. He expected as much, though, because whenever he spent time researching, he felt good. As Sandra often told him, research was his superpower. Something nobody ever talked about, however, was that using a superpower delivered a rush, filled a person with endorphins, and left the body feeling sturdy and strong. He thought it silly that mere research could do that for him, but it did. And this time was no exception.

Bouncing around the office, going over all that he had learned about Wilburn Walker, Max's fingers tingled. He expected Sandra in the next few minutes, and he wanted to make sure everything went right. Not only did he have a lot to tell her, but at one point during the day, he took a break to buy a bottle of wine because he planned to re-connect with his wife. They needed time together. Simple as that. Time to talk, to drink, to remember that life meant more than running one errand after another, chasing one job after another, putting out one fire after another.

"About time you got your head on right," Drummond said after hearing Max's intentions. "It's what I've been trying to tell you. Take me and Irene, for example. We've been meeting regularly ever since that fire department haunting. Once a week, we get together and talk about life as a ghost and life as a psychic. It's good to have somebody that understands you. That's what makes a good marriage, after all. And that's why you and Sandra have always been good together. When you don't have your head up your ass, that is."

Max was too jazzed up about his afternoon that he didn't even bother with a witty reply. His heart pattered away like a virgin teenager waiting to pick up a date — his first date. He heard a car door slam outside, and he checked the clock. Might be her.

"Good luck, partner," Drummond said before drifting into the built-in bookcase — his main home.

A few moments later, the office door opened and in walked his beautiful wife — along with the two boys, PB and J. His heart sank. He cringed. He loved those boys, but of all nights for his mother to not watch over them. At least, when he gazed upon Sandra, she smiled back.

"You have a good afternoon?" he asked.

"I saw some great houses. Real affordable, too. I've got pictures to show you, and I've got two of the places set for us to visit, and the third is having an open house this weekend, so we can go then. I thought we could show the boys what we're looking at, and maybe they'd want to come with us."

"I want to come," J said.

Shoving J, PB said, "I better go, too. Otherwise, nerd here will claim the best bedroom."

Sandra pointed at PB with a stern glare. "I warned you once already. Stop picking on your brother. We all had a rough morning today, and we're going to be together tonight, away from that apartment. A change of scene will do us all some good. We can even sleep in the office, so tomorrow will be different, too."

Drummond popped his head out of the bookcase. "What? No. This is my home. I don't want a bunch of noisy kids being kids all night long."

Max chuckled. Perhaps it was seeing Drummond upset

over something so minor. Perhaps it was his excitement over sharing his research. Or perhaps, his heart lightened as he watched the boys — their boys — getting situated on the couch like children readying for a bedtime story.

The Sandwich Boys loved Max's research stories. PB reveled in the gruesome parts while J liked trying to solve the puzzles. Lifting his gaze from the boys to Sandra, Max felt a new kind of warmth for her. When she smiled back at him, that warmth flooded over every inch of his body. He watched her face, wanting to memorize each line in her mouth, each sparkle in her eyes, each strand of her hair. He never wanted to forget this.

"Can we have popcorn?" PB asked.

Drummond swiped his hand through the air. "I draw the line there. It's bad enough having these kids ruin my evening but having them eat in front of me is too much."

Sandra said, "We don't have any popcorn."

"Well, that's good."

"But we do have some carrot sticks." She pulled out a small sandwich bag filled with sliced carrots. Neither boy raced to get the snack. Instead, they scrunched their faces as if somebody had passed gas. When that failed to change circumstances, they looked to Max for help.

Drummond laughed. "I retract my complaints. Let them eat carrots."

Before the lack of munchies became a bigger issue, Max raised his hands. "Okay, okay. Everybody pay attention. It's storytime."

"I'm only sticking around because it's for the case," Drummond said, slipping higher into the air until he reached the ceiling.

Max looked to Sandra but she only shrugged. Not wanting to lose the attention of his captive audience, Max said, "There are a few things odd about this case. The biggest one being that I still don't know how the story I'm going to tell you connects to the woman we found at the hotel. But another odd thing is how easy it was to find the story. I searched the name Wilburn Walker and within no time I had the basics. That's not normal for the kinds of cases we handle."

Drummond said, "That tells us that we need to be reading between the lines. Whatever the connection, it won't be obvious from the surface level. We need to pick up the small details and focus on the nuances."

Max wanted to tell his partner to have some patience because there were some very blatant and obvious holes in the story that he would get to, but not only were the Sandwich Boys sitting right there, he also did not want to say anything that might dissuade Drummond from continuing his rapt attention.

"So what happened already?" PB said. "A poisoning? Or maybe somebody got tied to their bed and lit on fire."

Max grimaced. "I need to have a talk with my mom about what she's been teaching you." He paused long enough to regain quiet in the room. Then, as if telling a ghost story over a campfire, Max delved into his tale. "June 20, 1891. It's a Saturday night, and a man named Henry Goins is getting into bed with his children. It's almost midnight. They lived here in Winston and because Henry's wife, Mary, worked long days, they did not have dinner until very late. By the time she finished with her house chores, everybody was already trying to get to sleep. Since it was Saturday night, there was a big commotion going on outside, lots of noise, so it was difficult to actually sleep. And then there came a knock at the door."

Bouncing, PB said, "Uh-oh. That's going to be trouble."

"It was. I imagine as Mary Goins grumpily got out of bed, part of her was scared. Bad enough they had somebody knocking on their door near midnight, but the Goins were a black family living in the 1890s here in North Carolina. Nothing good could come from such a late night visit, and I have no doubt she came up with some very terrible ideas of what might happen. But the knocking continued.

"She asked who was at the door, and a man's voice replied that it was Wilburn Walker. The man was freaking out. He begged for her to let him in, said there were men trying to kill him.

"Now, a lot of this story comes from testimony in court records as well as old editions of a newspaper called *People's Press*. So, remember, what we're hearing is a mixture of eyewitness testimony and journalistic suppositions. Because of that, it's not really clear if Mary or Henry knew Wilburn Walker, but she did go to the door, and for whatever reason, she opened that door."

Sandra sat on the couch between the boys. She put an arm around each one. "I know you two would never be so foolish."

J said, "Course not. But in Mary's case, it was a long time ago. Maybe they didn't teach their kids back then not to talk to strangers."

"We were a lot more trusting back in the day," Drummond said.

"Maybe," Sandra said. She gave J a squeeze and kissed the top of his head.

Max marveled that the boy did not try to squirm away. In fact, he appeared to like the affection. He had seen this from the boys before — particularly with his mother — but not often with Sandra.

Max continued, "Well, she did open the door. Three men were on the porch and they were swearing at each other, yelling and making a huge commotion. Mary snapped at them, told them to leave, she didn't want anything to do with whatever their argument was about, but she never got to complete her sentence. The instant the door opened far enough, Walker shoved his way inside and was followed by another man — this guy went by the entirely original name of John Smith."

PB and J laughed. Sandra rolled her eyes, but Max had not intended the joke for her.

"With all this fuss going on," he said, "perhaps nobody noticed the third man who walked in. He was small, wore a straw hat and a suit, and nobody knew who he was. But he pushed open the door all the way, whipped out a gun, and started shooting."

J said, "Really? Just like that?"

"Yup. Didn't say anything, didn't threaten anybody, just walked in and started shooting. Wilburn Walker spins around and, according to Henry Goins, the guy starts shooting 'as fast as he could pull the trigger.' Henry hears gun blasts and leaps across the bed, trying to shield his kids with his own body.

"Just so we're clear — this is not a wealthy house in the 1890s. In other words, it's small. There is a shootout going on in what was probably a one or two room house. Not a lot of places to hide. The only thing that saved those kids — besides their father — was the limited technology of guns at the time. They didn't have an Uzi that could spit out dozens of rounds in a breath or two."

"Just a six shooter, right?" PB said.

"Probably. Nobody reported on the types of guns used in the crime — it wasn't considered a big deal back then — but Walker would later say he only had three rounds in his gun when it all started. Anyway, fairly quickly the shooters run out of bullets, and everything goes quiet. This short man with the straw hat who started the whole thing, he runs away. Walker takes a look around and decides that running makes a lot of sense. He books off, too.

"Because Henry had his attention focused on protecting the kids, he failed to notice until afterward that his beloved Mary had been hit. He rushed over to her, wrapped her in his arms, and maybe tried to stop the bleeding. But a few minutes later, she was dead. Henry rushes outside, screaming *Murder! Murder!*

"Soon after that, the house is filled up with police and nosy neighbors. From their first inspection of the scene, they found Mary dead in the one room, and in the back room, they found John Smith also dead. With bullets flying all over the place and a lack of the forensic advances we have today, the police had no way to figure out whose bullet actually killed Goins or Smith."

The boys inched towards the edge of the couch, their eyes wide, as they listened to every word Max said. Sandra leaned back, smiling at the boys' reaction while also focusing on the story as it pertained to the case. Even Drummond listened closer than usual.

Outside, a car horn blared away. Somebody's music thumped a deep bass line. The rumble of an airliner passing overhead filled in the gaps. But it had all become a background wash to Max's audience. He wondered if stage actors felt the same way — a strange sense of joy mixed with nervous energy at having all the attention on the story he tried to tell.

"It didn't take long for an arrest." Max scooted onto his desk and let his feet dangle. "Wilburn Walker had originally identified himself at the door when he knocked, so Walker did not make any effort to hide. Smith was dead. That left the mystery man who started all the shooting. But they couldn't find him.

"Within short order, a trial was put together. The

courthouse overflowed with residents of all types. With Mary Goins being a black woman and John Smith a white man, the case took hold of everybody's interest.

"Most of the testimony was your standard fare, nothing too exciting. But Wilburn Walker gave testimony, too — something I doubt would happen today. No modern lawyer would dare let Walker speak unless there was no other choice. Not only that, but his testimony was printed up a few days later in *People's Press*."

"The whole thing?" Sandra asked.

"I think so." Max leaned back and grabbed a few sheets of paper he had printed out from a website. "Let's see here. He says: *Mr. Smith and myself came by Lee Wilson's between ten and eleven o'clock. There was a big crowd sitting on the porch there.*"

Drummond tapped his chin as he thought. "That must be where all the Saturday night partying was going on."

"*I said to Smith to go on. Smith said, let's go in. Pretty quick they all got up and went in the house and shut the door on us. This made Smith mad and he used some pretty bad words.*"

J frowned. "He's trying to pin it all on Smith."

"That's not a bad idea," PB said. "Smith is dead. He can't say crap."

"Let me finish," Max said, rattling the paper. "Basically, Smith is angry because they were turned away by this party and he goes mouthing off. Then Walker and Smith head out. But a few minutes later, according to Walker, four men from Wilson's house follow them and then call them over. Listen here: *I told Smith to come on and not have any fuss. The men (every one of whom were strangers to me) pushed on us so tight that I said to Smith fer us to go in at Goins' and stay there until the men went away.*"

Sandra perked up. "Doesn't that mean that Walker knew the Goins family? Otherwise, why would he think they'd let him in at such a late hour?"

"Good point." Max jotted the note down. "As Walker is banging on the door, the unidentified man comes up. *I knocked at the door, but before we could get in the man with the straw hat came up and said to Smith: 'Wasn't you the man that was over yonder at that house a few minutes ago?' Smith said he reckoned not. The stranger said, 'yes, you are, I've watched you all the way, and I'm going to shoot you.' That man had his pistol pointing at Smith all the time.*"

"That's convenient," Sandra said. "Walker says he had nothing to do with anything, and anybody who could corroborate is dead."

"Yeah, he doesn't strike me as too reliable. But he was all anybody had. He goes on to describe the shootout, says he witnessed Straw Hat kill Mary Goins, and then there's this: *It was dark in the room and if I hit Smith I don't know it.*"

Drummond snickered. "Either Walker is one smart fella or his shyster is."

As Max paused to let his words sink in, PB shrugged. "I don't get it. What's the big deal?"

"Walker is saying that maybe he did kill Smith," Max said, "but if he did, it was all an accident. Turned out to be a slick move, but that's jumping ahead. As the trial progressed, there was some evidence given about John Smith. He was a railroad bridge builder who lived near High Point, and from the trial transcripts, he was said to be a man who liked his alcohol too much and hung out with the wrong sorts of people even more.

"In the end, Wilburn Walker was cleared of charges. They said that it was obvious his bullet was not the one to kill Mary Goins. As for Smith, they had no way to know who killed him, but the court decided that if Walker was guilty of Smith's death, there was little doubt it was an accident. Just like Walker said."

J shook his head. "I bet you anything if Walker had been

black, they'd have strung him up before the day was out."

"Probably. You know as well as anybody that justice is not your best friend."

"Yeah, but it's still crappy to see it."

Max and Sandra had muddled through a few conversations together about handling racial issues with J. Until they could figure out a better way to approach things — if there was one — they had decided to simply offer the blunt truth. They would do their best to protect him, to prepare him, and to educate him. But they could not change the entire country's bias. In the end, the best they could do was offer their love.

Rocking in his seat, PB said, "Is that it? Walker goes free? What about Straw Hat man?"

Max kicked out his feet and nodded. "I've been wondering the same thing. See, Walker was set free, but part of the deal was that he had to appear in court as a witness, if they found the guy. Ten days later, the police had arrested two men they thought were connected to the crime — a guy named Charles Crutchfield and another guy, William Fansler. They might have been part of the group that followed Walker and Smith toward the Goins' house. Anyway, Walker was brought in along with a bunch of other witnesses, but ultimately, there was nothing of substance to convict the two men. They were set free. After that, the case went cold. No arrests, no suspicions, no investigation. And Straw Hat — he disappeared."

Max hopped down to his feet. He knew his audience was disappointed. But this wasn't a movie. The police did not always win. Circling the air above them, Drummond said, "Obviously, this third man with the straw hat, this mystery man, is significant. Unless, he's not — after all, the witch had Wilburn Walker's name on the paper. Maybe she wanted to ask Walker about Straw Hat. Could have been trying to find out who the mystery man was. Then of course — "

"I don't have any answers," Max said. "I've only been researching today and that's as far as the story goes."

"Then kick these kids out of here, and we can get to work. I've seen you pull all-nighters before. Let's work this case hard."

Max hesitated as he watched Sandra and the boys on the couch. He felt an odd thrill at the sight. They were his family. The four of them had yet to gel completely, yet they were on their way. The craziness of the past months had formed cracks, but it hadn't destroyed them.

Time to start fixing this, he thought. It stung that their date would be postponed, but these boys needed a night out, too.

"That's all for storytime, but I think you had the right idea. Let's get some popcorn, pull up a movie on my laptop, and cozy up for the night."

"Really?" both boys asked with mouths open wide.

Sandra cocked an eyebrow. "Really?" She had to know that part of Max wanted to join Drummond and research the night away. Perhaps another part of her sensed that Max had planned something for her.

Max winked at her. "What's the point of all this work if not to enjoy our family?"

"Oh, come on," Drummond said. "That's not fair using my words against me."

As Sandra and the boys got their impromptu movie night ready, Max went to the bathroom. He motioned for Drummond to follow.

"I don't know what your sudden problem is with these kids, but that's enough." Max's firm scowl kept Drummond's snide comments at bay. "They are part of this family, so get comfortable with it."

"I didn't mean to insult you. I just ... it doesn't matter."

"As for the research, it's obvious that Wilburn Walker is important. He gets his name cast in a spell and suddenly two Mobleys are dead. We need to talk with him. Go back to the Other, use that network of ghosts you love to brag about and find him. Meet me back here at two in the morning. Once the boys are asleep, I'll hit the research hard. We'll get Sandra looking into that symbol from the dead women, too. Does that meet with your approval?"

Drummond nodded. "Sounds good."

"Gee, I'm so glad."

After a pause in which Max thought his partner would take their spat further, Drummond simply vanished. Max took a long breath and hoped things worked out even better than they sounded — because nothing sounded too good to him.

Chapter 9

MAX, SANDRA, AND THE SANDWICH BOYS enjoyed the evening until midnight rolled around. Though it took some prodding to get the hyped-up boys to go to sleep, once their heads hit the pillows, they crashed hard. As the peaceful night settled around them, Sandra rested her head on Max's shoulder.

"Are you going to try to get any rest before you start working?" she asked.

With the boys curled up in sleeping bags on the floor (Sandra thought of everything), Max figured he would be better off getting his work done before his energy waned. But no sooner did he get situated at his desk then he felt his eyelids grow heavy.

"How do you sleep like that?" Drummond asked.

Max startled. His eyes wide, his heart hammering, he tried to figure out where he was, and once he established that he was in the office, he needed to figure out what time it was. Two o'clock. The time he had agreed to meet with Drummond.

Snickering, the ghost said, "Should I let you sleep?"

"Hey, I'm mortal. I need rest."

"I'm actually kind of jealous. I'll never know again what it feels like to have a good night's sleep. The good news — it does mean I can do a lot of searching. The bad news — no luck in the Other. Wilburn Walker has never been there."

"Damn. I'd meant to try researching his story more, but obviously, I fell asleep."

"I didn't fail entirely. Once it was obvious that the guy wasn't in the Other, I had another idea. I went to visit Irene."

Rubbing the sleep from his eyes, Max said, "I thought we agreed no details of that kind of thing."

"Is everything a joke to you? Don't answer that. So I visited Irene because she's a psychic. A beautiful psychic but the focus here is on the psychic part. She speaks with the dead. Here's the important part — she can't speak to anything in the Other. Ghosts in the Other are separated from this world. That's kind of the draw for a lot of them. So, she has no way to communicate there. Witches can do it with spells but not a psychic."

Max's mind shifted into hyper-awareness as if he had gulped down three shots of espresso. "She found something. What? How?"

"Take a breath, pal. Being a psychic means she speaks with both ghosts on our plane, like me, and she can also speak with ghosts who've moved on. That's how real psychics can tell you what your loved ones are doing and all that kind of stuff. Get it?"

"Wilburn Walker moved on? And she spoke with him?"

Drummond shook his head. "She couldn't find him. He never moved on."

Max sat up. "He never moved on and he's never been to the Other."

"Exactly. Which means —"

"That he's still on this plane of existence as a ghost."

"That's what I'm thinking."

"If he's around here somewhere, can't Irene find him?"

"Oh, now you want her help." Drummond rocked on his heels that did not touch the ground. "I did ask her, but she couldn't make contact. He's not answering. That could mean a ton of things, but she said he is here. We just need to figure how to find him."

From the couch, in a groggy voice, Sandra whispered, "That's probably what your witch was after."

Max looked across the office. "You think that spell in the hotel was some kind of location spell?"

Sandra stretched her arms as she joined them. "Either that or it's the strangest summoning spell I've ever seen."

Max pulled over his laptop and tapped away at the keyboard. "If Wilburn Walker had been cursed, then somebody would know where that happened. He would've died in his home or on the road or somewhere and it would have been known by witches where to find him because clearly he holds some importance to the Mobleys and Mother Hope. And I don't believe for a second that those witches would forget where they cursed somebody." It took a breath of concentrated willpower not to rub his chest.

Drummond tapped his lips. "I can buy that. Which leaves the question — where did Walker go?"

"Presumably, he was buried like most people. I'm guessing he's in a cemetery."

Sandra squinted at Max. "No offense, but you might need some more rest. If Walker was buried in the cemetery, that would make it even easier for the witches to know his whereabouts."

"Only if they kept tabs on him. Bodies have been moved in the past. Cemeteries get lifted and changed locations when developers want land. And that's assuming they know exactly where he was buried to begin with. Considering all the trouble this guy is bringing down on our heads, I think it's safe to assume that nobody knows where he is. So, you can go to sleep, and Drummond, you can chill in your bookcase — I've got this. By morning, I'll know what cemetery to go to."

"How are you going to do that?" Drummond asked.

"It's me. I research."

It took Max close to three hours, but he did succeed. He skipped over all the obvious ways to find a grave — checking obituaries, contacting cemeteries, and looking for family plots. Surely, Mother Hope or Lena Mobley would have thought of that long before. Instead, he located all the cemeteries within a ten mile radius of Winston-Salem and started there. In some cases, he pulled up plot maps and simply went through every single name. In other cases, the cemeteries were more twenty-first century with searchable databases accessible online. That sped up his work. However, after several long and fruitless attempts, he realized that any online searchable cemetery would have been easy access for the witches, too. Yet while most cemeteries did not have complete, digitized data available, nearly every scrap of documented paperwork had been scanned into the internet. With the tedious and meticulous skills he used to go through census data from the early 1900s, Max approached the cemetery data as well.

Much of it was poorly scanned and in atrocious handwriting. In some cases, names and dates had been crossed out and the correct information squeezed in, barely legible. Other times, entries were blotted out, scratched out, or abbreviated. In one case, the name and date looked fine but the headstone location had been altered so many times that there was an arrow leading to the information scrawled in the margin. But Max stuck at it. By morning, he had brewed coffee, slurped down two cups, and sat at his desk with a satisfied smile.

Drummond flew in from the bookshelf. "You found him."

As PB and J took turns in the bathroom washing up, Sandra said that she would stay behind and make sure the boys got to school. Max explained that the cemetery would be a bit of a drive, and Sandra added that if necessary, she would pick up J from school, too.

Drummond tipped his hat at Sandra. "Don't worry, doll. I'll be there to help Max out."

An hour later, after Sandra drove the boys off to their full day of education, Max walked out to his car with Drummond at his side. As he opened the car door, he thought he saw a cloaked woman dashing around the corner.

"Is it just me, or have we been watched by that witch for a few days now?" Max asked.

"You saw her, too? She might be hoping you'll do her work for her. Find Wilburn Walker so she won't have to."

"You know what really bugs me about her?"

"That she's a witch? That she's spying on us? That she's the cause of flaring up this witch war? Take your pick."

Max got in the driver's seat and stared at the corner as if she might reappear and blow her cover. "It's the idea that she was having an affair with Mr. Berkley. I mean, for whatever stupid reason, he's unhappy in his marriage and wants to fool around — but why is she messing with him? What does he offer her?"

Drummond gazed off at the same spot. "If we're lucky, Walker will be able to fill in some gaps for us. Then we'll have a better idea of how the start of this fits in with the rest."

Turning over the engine, Max said, "Maybe you can teach me a little bit more about evading a tail today. I don't want that witch following us straight to Walker."

With a big grin, Drummond said, "Thought you'd never ask."

*   *   *   *

An hour later, after two wrong turns and a missed exit, Max finally reached the Oak Crest Cemetery. He had been to numerous cemeteries over the course of his career with the Porter Agency, but never before had he gone during daylight. Turned out, a daylight cemetery held an equal amount of disturbing energy as a nighttime cemetery. Mainly because Max's purpose had not changed — to talk with the dead.

It did not help that this particular cemetery had been abandoned for fifty years. The church it had been attached to burned down in 1982, and while several people maintained the graves for a few years afterward, eventually nobody put money into it anymore. Even the paved road winding through the woods to the church property had become a cracked, pothole-riddled mess.

Max got out of the car as Drummond said, "You really think Walker's here?"

"If he is, he'll be buried somewhere in the back with the oldest graves, but I could be wrong. Is there anybody around?"

Drummond angled his head as if to say *Are you serious?* After all, ghosts abounded in any cemetery.

They strolled through the rows of graves — some headstones knocked over, some chipped or cracked, some so weatherworn that the information could no longer be seen — and Max had to fight the urge to whistle. He guessed all the ghosts had heard jokes like that for ages. Drummond smiled in one direction, nodded in another, even waved to someone in the distance.

"Are you actually going to talk to anybody?" Max asked.

"Have some patience. There's etiquette involved. This is their permanent home. I can't just go barging in demanding answers. Not only that, but have you considered the fact that these ghosts are stuck here? If they could've moved on, they would've already done so."

"I hadn't thought of that. Sorry."

Drummond winked. "It's not really that bad. In fact, I see a redhead with curls that would be the perfect one to talk with. Be right back."

Max watched as Drummond drifted off three rows and leaned his elbow on a headstone with a small angel perched at the top. He tipped back his Fedora and spoke quietly. Like a high school football player leaning in on a cheerleader, he even over-laughed and reached out with a gentle graze of her shoulder. Of course, Max could not see the little redhead, but watching Drummond's performance felt like watching a trained actor demonstrating a scene-for-two without a partner.

"My life is not normal."

A moment later Drummond returned. "Nice gal. If she ever makes it out of here and gets to the Other, I told her to look me up."

"Does she know where Walker is?"

"That she does. Follow me."

Drummond cut across several rows, but Max could not pass through headstones, so he walked around. The soft ground smelled of rich earth, and he wondered how deep the coffins were buried so long ago. Without a backhoe to make the digging easy, did people prefer shallow graves? Did he have to worry about stepping on somebody? When he caught up, Drummond had already started a conversation with Wilburn Walker.

"This here is my partner, Max. He can't see you, but I can act as a translator for you. Is that okay?" After listening to the response, Drummond leaned toward Max. "He says it's okay."

Max tried to clear his mind. He imagined all the other ghosts forming a circle around them. An abandoned cemetery did not get many visitors, if any at all — this had to be one of the most exciting things to happen in a long time.

Looking in the same direction that Drummond had been talking, Max said, "Thank you for your time, Mr. Walker."

Drummond made a face like a parent on the verge of losing his patience. "He says he won't talk with us for free."

"What kind of payment does he want?" Ghosts had no need for money.

Drummond listened. Confused, he turned to Max. "Do you know what a *Jenga* is?"

Minutes later, Walker brought Max and Drummond to the old groundskeeper's shed. Apparently, a decade ago, several teenagers would hang out in the shed drinking beer, smoking cigarettes, and playing the old wood tower game. The ghosts were fascinated each time the kids played, but of course, the ghosts could not play unless they wished to cause themselves a lot of pain.

Drummond stared at the wood blocks. To Max, he said, "This is it? A bunch of building blocks? Isn't this what babies play with?"

"It was bit of a fad for a while."

"You people got real weird after I died. Anyway, Walker says that he'll tell us everything he can as long as you act as his hands and play the game for him and his friends."

Max made a short tour of the tiny shed. He checked the walls, the floor, and the ceiling for any sign of a casting circle or a witch's curse. Nothing suggested that Walker's request was anything more than what it appeared to be on the surface.

With a shrug, Max said, "Um, okay."

Drummond's attention turned toward the shed door. He suddenly straightened and a sly grin crossed his lips.

Max said, "Did your redhead just walk in?"

"A bunch of ghosts walked in. They want to see what's going on. Daphne just happens to be one of them."

"Daphne? You know her name now."

Drummond had his arm hanging in the air, and Max could only assume that his partner held Daphne's shoulder.

"Ready?" Drummond asked the empty space that was Walker. "Here we go. Ladies and gentlemen, it is my pleasure to present a game of Jenga — whatever that is — with Mr. Walker facing off against Mr. Randolph from 1962. Good luck, gentlemen. And the first move is Mr. Walker's. Max, he said he wants the middle one at the bottom."

Withholding any display of mirth, Max pointed to the wood block, and when he received confirmation, he slid it out. He placed it atop the tower.

"That's it?" Drummond said, shaking his head.

To Walker, Max said, "We appreciate you talking with us. We're interested in your case and how it pertains to current events."

"Mr. Randolph wants the block on the left side four from the bottom."

As Max performed the requested maneuver, he said, "I've read the testimony you gave in court about the murder of Mary Goins and John Smith, but that all seems rather straightforward. Certainly nothing to get a bunch of witches riled up. The only part I can think of that's still murky is the man in the straw hat."

Drummond made an odd face — one Max thought meant disappointment. "Walker's insisting on telling you his version of the story from the beginning. If you ask me, I think he wants to make sure this ridiculous game lasts as long as possible."

Max took a deep breath, noticing how musty the shed

smelled. It amazed him that the place remained standing. Weeds penetrated every crack on the floor and sunlight broke through every crack along the ceiling.

"As long as this place doesn't collapse on us, we can play."

With his chilly head close to Max's ear, Drummond said, "Don't forget that these ghosts have been here a long time. Don't piss them off. We don't want any of them losing their cool."

"How am I to do that? I can't even see them?"

"Just don't lose."

"But —"

Backing up, Drummond said, "Okay, Walker's turn. He wants the block seventh from the bottom on the right side."

For the next hour, Walker doled out his tale in dribbles. He refused to add anything until after each play of the game had been made. At first, Max gave little thought to the procedure. But as the tower grew taller and less sturdy, he wondered what might happen if the thing toppled over. Would that be the end of the interview? If Walker lost, would he take it out on Max? Drummond certainly thought so.

By the time Walker had reached the point of the story where he had been released from custody, a cold sweat had broken out on Max's brow. Both contestants had figured out the benefit to taking pieces off the sides. In short time, they had constructed a long vertebrae-like tower. It swayed with every brush of air. Even Max's breathing threatened to knock it down.

Wiping his damp hands against his pants, Max looked toward where he thought Walker floated. "This all brings us to our main point of interest — this mystery man. The one in the straw hat. According to all I could find, he disappeared and left you in the lurch. But since you don't seem to be too worried about all these witches looking for you, I'm thinking they've been looking for you in order to find him." That thought had not really occurred to Max until he spoke the words, but it sounded like a reasonable conclusion.

Apparently Walker thought so, too. Drummond said, "He wants to move the left block from that middle section."

Max circled the table until he thought he had a good angle on the piece. Licking his lips, he hunched over and concentrated on controlling his fingers. Gently, he nudged the woodblock halfway out. And then it caught.

Sweat dripped into his open mouth. The salty taste reminded him what the rest of his body already knew — this was not a simple game. His pulse throbbed against his temples. He stepped back and stretched his arms. Wanting nothing more than to ask Drummond how much was at stake by this move, he stared at the table in silence.

"You okay?" Drummond asked.

Max knew Walker watched him. Might even have made a bet on the outcome of the game. Lowering towards the tower once more, Max thought about Sandra. She would tell him to keep going forward. Play the game.

With a quick motion he snatched the block free and stood back. The tower swayed far to the side, but before it fell over, it swayed back until it found a new balance. Max laid the tile on top and stepped away from the table, afraid to even breathe in its direction.

"I'm ready for the answer to my question."

Drummond winked. But the amusement drained from his pale face leaving behind a concerned stare at Mr. Randolph. "Says the game ain't over yet." Drummond's head snapped towards Walker. "Now this nut is saying he decides when the game starts and when it finishes. Now they're both yelling at each other." Drummond drifted alongside Max. In a lower voice, he said, "I've heard about this kind of thing, but I've never seen it."

"What thing? What the hell is happening?"

"Some folks in the Other told me that ghosts stuck in cemeteries, especially ones that had been here a long, long time, well, they go a bit nutty. They develop grudges over minor matters and they come up with crazy deals over things you don't make deals about. In other words, they're all stuck together and are looking for ways to amuse themselves."

"You're saying that Mr. Walker made me play this game to settle some kind of disagreement that might have been going on for decades?"

"Give me a second. I'll find out what's going on." Drummond drifted off, bent his head down toward one corner of the shed, and a moment later returned. "Daphne's friend says that Randolph blames Walker for killing a tree that shaded his gravestone. She's not sure what the game had to do with any of it, though."

"I do," Max said. Waving his hands in the air, he said in a loud voice, "Everybody calm down. Stop this fighting." He glanced back at Drummond, and his partner nodded that things had stopped for a moment — all curious eyes on Max. "Mr. Walker, you need to step outside with my partner and me, right now."

Max glanced back and Drummond said, "He's using some colorful language to suggest where you can take your demand."

"In that case, Mr. Randolph, allow me to explain to you why Walker wanted to play this game."

Drummond popped up. "It appears Mr. Walker has decided that the three of us should talk outside, after all."

As Max started toward the door, he said, "Everybody else just stay here. We'll be right back to finish the game."

Once they were outside, Max made sure they walked several feet away from the door — he had no idea how good a ghost's hearing could be but had no intention of aiding eavesdroppers.

Drummond said, "Walker's here and wants to know what you've got to say. And frankly, I want to know what's going on with that game."

Max gestured to Drummond, asking where Walker stood. Drummond indicated the space toward his right.

"Don't get too excited," Max said to his partner. "There's nothing nefarious going on here. Like you said, these people have been cooped up here too long. I've seen it with my own boys. The one starts picking on the other for no reason. I mean those boys have been through so much together. They got each other's backs. Like partners. Yet, stuck with each other for a few months day in and day out, and the one is just pick-pick-picking at the other. I figure it's the same thing here. That right, Mr. Walker? You don't really care about Randolph. You just want to embarrass him. Have a little fun at his expense. It's amusing. So, along comes me — a living human being that wants information from you — and you think jackpot. You knew I would do everything I could to make sure you win. It wouldn't do me any good to have you lose, have you be in a bad mood, and then you won't help us."

Drummond said, "He's laughing."

"It is kind of funny. Especially because you are going to tell us everything we want to know right now, or I'll go back in there and see that you lose the game. I wonder how many decades Mr. Randolph will hold that loss over your head. I hear there are a lot of pretty ghosts around here. They might not be so interested if you fall flat in front of everybody, I mean, really, if you think about it, you've created a rather high-stakes game — for a ghost. One reputation versus another. You ain't got much else worth anything."

"He's not liking what you're saying, but I think he's ready to talk."

He did talk. A lot. He blubbered on about how he never actually knew Straw Hat, never knew where the guy came from, never knew his real name, never knew why he wanted to kill John Smith. But after all that had happened, Walker couldn't let it go.

At first, it haunted him in his dreams. He kept reliving the gunfight — the most frightening experience of his life. Kept seeing Mary Goins fall to the floor as guns roared in the air. So, he tried to find out what he could about the men who had attacked him and Smith. That didn't go very well.

Drummond said, "He says he's no good at finding things out. Not that bright a guy."

Walker continued for several years with no success. Poking around here and there. Whenever he thought he had a lead, he'd do his best to follow it up, but it all amounted to nothing. Until one day in late-1904, an odd thing happened.

Way out across the country in Bakersfield, California, a strange man entered the county jail. He asked for the Sheriff. When the Sheriff approached, the man said that he had committed a murder in Winston, North Carolina. Said it happened sixteen years ago and that he had committed the crime with three other men. This strange fellow called himself William Crutchfield.

When Walker heard about it, he thought this surely was the guy. But, in the end, his excitement at the news waned. The guy was in California and a rumor had floated around that this William Crutchfield dabbled in witchcraft. Walker admitted to having committed many sinful acts, but he would never risk his soul to such evil things. He decided to let the matter go. Even if Mary Goins' face still haunted his dreams.

Max wished he could see the ghost. Partly to judge the truthfulness of the statements made, partly because he wanted the satisfaction of seeing a haunted ghost. Drummond must have been thinking along similar lines because the ghost made a shoving motion and said, "What else about Crutchfield? What are you holding back?"

Max's phone rang — Sandra. He thought about letting it go to voicemail, but Sandra knew what he was doing. She wouldn't call casually. "What's the matter?" he answered.

"You need to get back now," she said.

"I'm a little busy at the cemetery."

"One of the Mobleys tried to pick up J from school."

The world skipped a beat. Another second went by as Max tried to get his lungs to fill up with air. At length, he said, "Be right there."

He turned to leave, but an icy wind passed through his chest.

Drummond said, "I don't think Walker will let you go until you finish the game."

"One of the Mobley coven tried to nab J."

"Crap." Drummond turned to Walker. "Look pal, we promise to come back and finish the game. But right now, we have an emergency to handle."

The cold brushed against Max's body again.

"You do that to my partner once more, and I'm going to knock you senseless in front of all the other ghosts," Drummond said, moving in quick.

Max raised a hand. "It's okay, it's okay. You want to win the game? Fine. Let's go."

They entered the shed. Max stepped toward the tower. "I believe it's Mr. Randolph's turn."

Drummond floated nearby. "Randolph says he wants the middle block from the third at the bottom."

Max pulled the block out with ease and smashed it on the top. Before all the wood blocks had finished rattling to the floor, he had left the shed. He never worried about the consequences.

Drummond had his back.

Chapter 10

MAX RACED AWAY FROM THE CEMETERY, the suspension on his car getting a full workout against the uneven pavement in the woods. When he broke free onto the main road, garnering angry honks from startled drivers, he pressed heavy against the gas pedal. Images of his arrival at the school whipped through his head — Sandra holding J, J pale and frightened, and social services standing over them with arms crossed and a disapproving scowl.

Drummond floated in the passenger seat, his hand gripping the door as if an accident would send him flying through the windshield. "You better slow down. You won't do your wife and boys any good if you end up dead before you even get to the school."

"The Mobley witches tried to kidnap my boy."

"That's right. And they did it to get to you. Don't do them a favor and make their job any easier."

Though his grip on the steering wheel did not ease, Max's foot backed off the gas pedal — a little. His head pounded with blood and he heard only his heartbeat. With a perplexed frown, he said, "This doesn't make any sense. It's a bad move on their part."

"Don't you worry about that. Nobody takes a shot at my people and gets away with it."

Max snatched a peek at his partner. Drummond's grim expression gave Max a taste of how imposing the man must have been when he was alive. Max said, "I thought you were all about calming me down."

"So you don't get into an accident. That doesn't mean

the Mobleys are off the hook."

Stopping at a traffic light, Max rubbed his jaw as he thought. "From the way things are going, I'm guessing that the cloaked witch is working for the Mobleys. Might even be a Mobley witch herself."

"They certainly seem to be the most interested in Walker."

"The way I see it, the cloaked witch was going to cast some kind of spell to find Walker. Her affair with Mrs. Berkley's husband was a side thing — unrelated. It was her bad luck that Berkley hired us."

Drummond gazed ahead as he digested the idea. "If she is a Mobley witch, then that would explain how Mother Hope found out about it all. With the escalating tensions between the two groups, I have to believe that Mother Hope has several Magi spying on the Mobleys."

Max flexed his fingers, his tension easing. "So, Mother Hope takes a preemptive hit on two of the Mobleys."

"Seems like it. The part I don't get is what any of this has to do with Walker."

Max turned onto the side road that led to the school. "That's because this is not about Walker."

"Right, it's Crutchfield."

"I think so. Walker told us that William Crutchfield began messing around with witchcraft. If you're living in the 1890s and you're messing around with witchcraft and you're living in the Winston area, then who are you most likely to come into contact with?"

Drummond nodded. "Grandma Mobley. No doubt about it."

"Her rivalry with Mother Hope has been going on a long time." Max pulled into the large parking lot and tucked into a space near the middle. "Do me a favor. When I can, I'm going to have to research about Crutchfield and figure out if he's actually Straw Hat. But it'll be a heck of a lot easier if you can find the guy floating around the Other."

"Consider it done. You sure you don't want me going to the Mobleys with you guys?"

"I'm calm enough now. And, frankly, I think the Mobleys have far more to fear from Sandra than they do from you or me."

Drummond chuckled. "Ain't that a fact."

As Max exited the car, Drummond vanished. Walking toward the school's entrance, Max moved with a confident stride. The anger that had propelled him while driving dissipated with each step. Drummond had been right. He needed to be calm and thinking straight. But when he opened the door and stepped into the school lobby, when he saw his wife and his son sitting on a wood bench by a cinderblock wall, a tsunami of emotions knocked through him.

He always had love and concern for his wife, and while the Sandwich Boys were new additions to their lives, he cared for them deeply. But the tableau they formed — the mother consumed with worry and anger, the son trying to hide his fear — struck Max different than before. The word *family* had been thrown about often, and he knew they meant it every time they said it, yet here, sitting anxiously, waiting impatiently, he glimpsed a shard of that special jewel. Mother and son clinging to each other for security and for support. Separate people forming a single unit. Family.

Sandra jumped to her feet and headed off Max before he could say a word. "Everything is okay here — now. Apparently, a woman came in and attempted to give a story as to why she was there to pick up J. She gave her name as Christine Mobley. The school, of course, had no record of her being authorized and refused to help her. She left. No trouble made."

"It was a threat."

"I think so, too. They're telling us they know where J goes to school. If they really wanted to take him, they would never have left a Mobley name. Unless it's the Magi and they want to set up the Mobleys."

"After hanging two of their witches, I don't see why the Magi would bother with subtle threats to us. Plus, Mother Hope has me cursed. She's got the ultimate threat hanging over me."

With a grim nod, Sandra said, "I had the same thoughts. Kind of hoped you'd come up with a different conclusion, though. But it sounds like we agree — the Mobleys are behind this."

"They're threatening our family." Max gazed over at J. The boy caught his eye and gave a thumbs-up. "I have a bunch to tell you — we met Wilburn Walker — but it can wait. We need to deal with that coven right now."

"I was thinking the same thing. But I've got this," Sandra said, her eyes focused in a dark manner that chilled Max's skin. "You take J back to your mom's place."

She turned to leave, but Max said, "No."

Swiveling back on him, she said, "You don't get to handle everything. I am the one who has studied witches. I know them better than you. Let me take care of this."

"Not alone. We do this together."

"That sounds great, but you're forgetting something — J."

Max waved the boy to join them. "We're bringing him with us. He needs to see who these people are. Even if he doesn't believe in them, he has to be prepared — just in case."

Sandra observed Max's face for a moment before accepting the idea. As they turned to leave, Max heard a throat being cleared echo off the cinderblock walls.

Before he turned back, before he saw the principal standing in the office doorway, he had a sudden energy surge through his nerves. It took him a half-second to recognize it — the sensation of being caught doing something wrong at school.

Principal Hardy strutted across the hall, her heels making sharp clicks on the tile. "Mr. Porter, it seems we keep meeting under less than pleasant circumstances."

"Not a problem today. Nobody got harmed, and from what I understand, you all did a great job protecting our son. We appreciate it."

He started to leave, but she said, "I would like to discuss the incident with you. To make sure we are all on the same page."

Max smirked. "I promise you we are not interested in a lawsuit against the school. Nothing bad happened. No harm, no foul."

"Not that I was purposefully listening in, but I did hear some of your discussion with your wife. I don't want to let you go causing problems with other people because of what happened here."

"Is there some kind of waiver that you want me to sign? Is that what this is about?"

Principal Hardy tugged her blouse tight as if setting armor to cover the proper vital points. "I assure you, Mr. Porter, my interests are only in the safety and welfare of J. The school is not afraid of liability nor do we need you to sign a waiver because we have done nothing wrong. Everything is documented and clearly we did the right thing. Part of our procedure is to sit down with the parents and inform you in detail about the incident, let you read the reports, and have you sign off on them, so that we are all in agreement."

Max pulled out a Porter Agency business card from his wallet and handed it over. "Call my office and make an appointment. We'll come in and handle all of your paperwork. But right now, my family needs to be together. And that's what we're going to do."

Max, Sandra, and J walked out.

J stayed quiet the entire drive to the Mobley house. Max figured the boy could sense the tension radiating from Sandra. He was a survivor. He knew the best way to get through the next few hours — eyes open, ears clear, mouth closed.

Max had never learned such a lesson growing up. Would have saved him a lot of trouble. As they pulled into the development where the Mobleys lived, he said, "Honey, I know you're upset, but —"

"You should be upset, too."

"I am. All I wanted to say —"

"If you have anything to say, it should be to Lena Mobley. But don't bother. I got it covered."

Before Max parked the car in the driveway, Sandra had the passenger-side door open. She stormed across the yard and up onto the porch. Banging on the door and punching the doorbell, she stood firm as an iron pike.

Max turned back to J. "The women in this house can be dangerous. They won't look it. In fact, they look pretty old and dowdy, but trust me. You do not want to mess with these people."

J's brow pulled down. "You mean like Sandra is about to do?"

"As tough as these women are, they got nothing when compared to Sandra — especially when she's ticked off."

J shivered out a grin. "I can believe that."

"Stay close to me. Don't go wandering off, and don't say a word to any of the women. I mean it. They can do a lot to hurt you with any little bit of information you may give. Even things you don't think matter — they matter. Understand?"

J nodded with such trepidation that Max actually believed he had gotten through to the boy. They hurried to catch up with Sandra. As they approached the porch, the front door opened — no telling how many times Sandra had pushed the doorbell — and Jessica Mobley stood in the entranceway.

Among the youngest of the Mobley coven, Jessica had a waifish appearance. But Max had seen her in action before — fast, vicious, loyal, and perhaps one of the least forgiving witches he had ever come across.

Sandra pushed her arm against Jessica's chest and shoved the girl out of the way. As Max and J jogged to catch up, Sandra burst into the living room — no longer housing two corpses, it had returned to its normal purpose of entertaining.

"What you did was indecent and stupid," Sandra said to Lena Mobley.

Lena sat in her high-backed chair with a book in her lap. She made no attempt to appear cordial. In fact, as Max reached the open archway into the living room, he saw a deep scowl appear on the woman's face that could quell a rabid dog. "You want to think carefully about who you call stupid — especially as you are the one barging into a witch coven."

"Coming after my boy is the wrong move."

"I don't know what you think we've done, and I don't care. Only because you and your husband have helped us out in the past will I afford you this courtesy — turn around and leave right now. I will forget this intrusion."

Clenching her fists, seething with fiery rage, Sandra strode right up to Lena and pressed her foot on the arm of the chair. With a sharp shove that screeched the chair legs against the floor, she said, "You don't get to go after my boy and then act like you're doing me a favor. You do not want me as an enemy."

Lena popped to her feet. Max reached into his pocket, his hand settling on the grip of his handgun. He looked to his side, checking that J had not wandered off, and then stepped back slightly to make sure that Jessica Mobley did not have access to J. For her part, Jessica casually closed the front door and sauntered into the living room, taking a gentle seat on the far end of the couch. She crossed her legs and watched as if taking in an afternoon drama on television.

Despite the calmness in her voice, every facet of Lena's physical being screamed her desire to throttle Sandra to death. "I can see that you are quite upset. Clearly you think that we had something to do with trouble that came to your son. We did not. We have far more pressing matters to worry about than what goes on in the Porter lives. We've been attacked by our enemy. What makes you think I care one iota about the sewer rats you've adopted?"

But Sandra had gone too far into an ardent defense of her family. Max could tell she heard nothing. Sandra stabbed the air in front of Lena. "If you ever come to my son's school again, if you ever send anybody even remotely near my boys, I will not only kill you, but I will kill every single member of this coven. Even if I have to sell my soul to do it."

The kitchen door on the back wall opened, and the most frightening sight Max could have seen stepped forth — a frail, ninety pound woman, stark white hair, skin wrinkled and hanging from over a hundred years of life. Grandma

Mobley.

She wore thick, heavy shoes that made each slow step hit with a resounding clump. It reverberated around the room as if amplified by hidden microphones. Sandra and Lena's argument ceased. Jessica jolted to her feet, smoothing down her clothes and tossing her hair back to make the best impression.

When Grandma Mobley turned toward Max, his mouth dried and he heard J gasp — the boy had seen how one of her eyes clouded over milky-white. Max felt J's hand clutch the back of his coat.

After only a half-dozen steps, Grandma Mobley halted. She surveyed the room with her one good eye before turning her focus onto Sandra.

Drawing on her deep well of gumption, Sandra took a step forward. "I've never seen you looking so ..."

"Alive?" Grandma Mobley tittered. "My sisters in the coven have worked their best to help me along. The kind of magic that keeps you young — I never liked to mess with it too much. It can become addictive. Just ask Mother Hope. And it's a case of diminishing returns. Very destructive to the body in the long run."

With a worried glance at Jessica, Lena said, "We apologize for the disruption."

"No need. Sometimes it's healthy to have a little arguing. It helps put things in perspective. And from what I'm hearing, the Porters need a strong dose of perspective."

Sandra glowered at Lena even as she spoke to Grandma Mobley. "You tell your sisters that coming after my boys is off the table. They do that again —"

"And I'll thank them." Grandma Mobley waited until Sandra's attention returned. "I don't care what you think is going on, but the Magi have instigated a terrible battle of wills between us. Terrible for them, of course, because I have the greatest willpower of any witch in this state. Probably this country. I have lived too long and seen too many things to simply bow to Mother Hope."

Rolling her shoulders back and straightening her spine, Grandma Mobley walked over toward Max and J. She moved faster, more assuredly, and with each step it became clearer that any signs of age were mere artifice.

J shrunk behind Max. Grandma Mobley chuckled.

"Come out here, boy."

Max inched closer to Grandma Mobley. "You don't want to do this."

"I will do whatever I see fit. We are about to fight a very powerful enemy and when it comes to you and your family, we don't care. Unless you've decided to join us. Allies are always given our great appreciation."

Through a tight jaw, Sandra said, "You want to fight the Magi, then you go right ahead. But there is no reason to involve us."

"Naïve. You really think you can spend the last bunch of years playing in our pond, working with the Hulls, working with the Magi, working with us — you really think you can do that and suffer no consequences?" She sniffed in the direction of J. "This boy is full of youthful energy. A lot of spells call for such a thing."

In the most vicious tones Max had ever heard, Sandra said, "Touch him and I'll tear out your one good eye."

Grandma Mobley grinned — a wet, hideous twisting of her lips. "I believe you would. Of course, sometimes that's necessary for a powerful spell. And that's what I want you to remember. You, your family, your kids, your life is in this battle. Mother Hope wants to try to take me down. She's been wanting to do it for decades. And she always fails. Do you know why? Because I have the greater will. I have the strength to go to the darkest reaches, further than any other. You think you're strong enough to stand up to me to protect your boy? You're nothing. You have no idea what I'm capable of doing to protect my coven."

Max noticed that Grandma Mobley had kept one hand at her side most of the time. With a jerk, that hand clenched tight. Max understood as those fingers closed that while she had been making her speech, part of her had also been casting a spell. He had never seen such a thing before. To be able to concentrate enough to cast a spell while also holding a conversation — a heated one, at that — turned his stomach.

As the next thought hit Max — what spell was she casting? — Jessica flew backwards into the wall. She wriggled like a trapped bug. Held several inches off the floor as if by a huge brute, she groaned. Mascara ran down her face with her tears.

Lena glared at the young woman, her anger eager to have a safe place to unload. "What did you do?"

Jessica tried to speak but only strained gurgles came out.

With a flick of her wrist, Grandma Mobley opened her hand, and Jessica dropped to the floor. "Do we understand each other?"

Gasping, Jessica said, "Yes, yes. I'm so sorry."

"Go get yourself cleaned up."

Max said, "What was that for?"

Grandma Mobley put one hand on her hip. "Stop concerning yourself with my affairs. Collect your wife and your boy and go home. If you really want us to leave you alone, then leave this situation alone. Because the next time I see you, you'll either be prostrating before me or begging for mercy — and we both know that mercy will never come." Turning away, she snapped her fingers at Lena. "After our guests leave, please make some of your tea. We have a lot to discuss."

Chapter 11

HEADING BACK WAS A SOLEMN AFFAIR. They watched the road and listened to the sounds of other cars rolling by. Max refrained from checking the rearview mirror. If J had a thousand-yard stare, Max did not want to see it.

As the minutes ticked by, the silence took on weight. It grew thick in the air and pressed down on Max's shoulders. Without changing position, he spoke barely above a whisper. "I need to research this new guy — William Crutchfield." He thought he caught Sandra nodding out of the corner of his eye.

He tried to think of something to say to J, some parental wisdom or simple explanation that might help the boy understand what they had all experienced. But until J accepted that witches and ghosts and magic existed, nothing Max said would suffice. Heck, even if J accepted all those things, it would still be difficult.

From the backseat, in a voice so soft that Max had a hard time believing it came from J, the boy asked, "What did that lady do? She going to be okay?"

With his eyes on the road, Max said, "Jessica? She'll be fine. You have to think of those ladies as one big family. The old woman is like their parent. Sometimes a parent has to punish her kids in order to teach them a lesson. Right? So the kids learn about consequences. Jessica must've done something to upset Grandma Mobley. So she's paying the consequences. But loving parents don't go out of their way to hurt their children, and I don't think Grandma Mobley would either." Max hoped that was true.

"What did she do wrong?"

Sandra said, "We're never going to know. It's not our business, and it's not our problem."

"And why did she do that in front of us?" J asked.

Max said, "To make a point."

J said nothing more. When they got to Mrs. Porter's apartment, he rushed off to the back room and closed the door. Mrs. Porter had been sitting on the couch with PB watching television. She looked up at Max and Sandra.

"What's wrong?"

Max said, "Nothing."

Sandra placed her hand on Max's chest. "He'll be fine. I'll talk to him later. Those witches scared him a little more than he could handle."

"I should've known not to bring him."

"It's a lot to take in."

"I thought he could handle it. I thought they wouldn't do anything in front of him." Max kissed Sandra and headed to the door. He stopped before opening it. The taste of her lips played against his — a hint of cherry. He inhaled and smelled her fragrance — wildflowers.

Turning back, he placed his hand on her shoulder. With a quizzical turn of her head, she looked up at him like a perfect shot in a romance movie. He winked. To his mother, he said, "Sandra and I need to go out. We'll be back in a few hours. That okay?"

"Of course," Mrs. Porter said. "It's not like I have any plans. I don't have a life of my own with my own things to do and my own friends to see. I love sitting here taking care of your kids."

She delivered her speech in her usual cheery, passive-aggressive manner. For that, Max was thankful. Normally, such a tactic would fill him with dread and send him in a nervous attempt to placate his mother. But this time, he decided to simply take her words at face value because he needed to.

"Thanks, Mom."

Before she could start any kind of follow up, he opened the door and escorted his wife out. As they walked to the car, Sandra said, "What's this all about?"

"We are going on a date." Before she could protest, he pressed his mouth against hers. When he pulled back, he said, "J is not the only one shaken up by what we saw. If Grandma Mobley and Mother Hope are going to escalate their feud, then we may never get a chance to date again. You and I need to spend time together — time that doesn't involve being parents and that most certainly doesn't involve witches. It's that simple. Either we take advantage of the moment we have, or we get screwed — and not in a good way."

Sandra gave a thoughtful nod. Then as his words settled in her head, she snorted a laugh. "Okay, let's go."

Less than an hour later, Max parked the car in the lot of a dentist's office on Westgate Center Drive. He and Sandra squirmed into the backseat and popped the cork on a bottle of wine. She opened a Wendy's take-out bag and they set up a nighttime picnic.

"I know what you're doing," she said with a playful warning in her voice. "But wine and Wendy's only goes so far."

Max handed her a plastic cup of wine. "I'm not trying to suggest that one night is going to fix everything. But I think we both can agree that things between us right now are pretty crappy. If we don't start working at it, it's only going to get worse. And with all that's happening around us, we need to be on the road toward getting better."

"I hate that we have to have these talks. You'd think after all these years, we would've learned by now how to avoid getting into these grumpy, nitpicking, downtimes."

"Oh, I'm pretty sure marriage never stops having ups and downs. The point is that we go through it together."

Pouting in a way that Max found adorable, Sandra said, "Why does it have to be so hard, though? I mean, we know witches and we know magic. You'd think we'd be able to put that to good use and avoid all the downs in our relationship."

Max chuckled. "Like a never-ending happiness spell?"

"Exactly."

"I'll get on that right away."

She raised her plastic cup. "To abusing magic for the purpose of easing our marriage." Max touched his cup to hers and they drank. Gazing around the empty parking lot, she asked, "So why are we here?"

"You don't recognize this place?"

"Of course I recognize it. Across the street is where Doctor Connor practiced — both optometry and witchcraft."

"For me, this is where it all began. I know that technically it began in our old office with Mr. Modesto hiring us for the Hulls and all of that, but initially, that was just a weird job to make money. But here, at Doctor Connor's office, here's where I really started to get a taste of what we were in for."

"I would've thought seeing Drummond the first time did that for you."

"It did, but he's a friend. Here is where the danger began. Doctor Connor was my first witch."

Sandra grinned. "You never forget your first."

"Through it all — all the spells and summoned souls, all the witchcraft and ghosts — it's been the two of us.

Together. You and me. That's how we've survived. But lately, this awful distance between us is making me feel like I'm standing on my own. And with what we saw today, we can't be separated, can't be on our own."

Taking a bite of her burger, Sandra spoke while chewing. "What did you expect? Our problem — our non-witch problem, that is — is we're stuck living with your mother."

"We've faced the Hull family. We've faced powerful covens. We've faced magic and death. Why should my mother be this big of a problem?"

Sandra startled at Max's words as if she had received an electric jolt. "Are you telling me that you think this is all about living with your mother?"

"Isn't that what you just said?"

"No. I mean, yes, but that's not what I mean."

As Max attempted to decipher Sandra's words, he slung back his cup of wine and refilled it. "So, it's not my mother?"

"It's us. Like you said — we've always faced these things together. And we've always had a specific way of handling our problems. Right?"

Max nodded, knowing the exact words she expected to hear. "Straight on through."

"Exactly. We don't dance around things, and we don't slough them off. We barrel straight through. Sometimes it's messy, but it has always served us well. But our last case — I don't know what it was that got to you, but you've changed. Maybe it was our house burning down or maybe your jealousy over Peter — who, remember, is gay and not a threat to you. I don't know what it is, but suddenly you're not there by my side pushing through our problems."

"I haven't gone anywhere."

"You haven't moved forward, either. I know you're not happy with all of us crammed together in your mother's apartment — I'm certainly not, either — but you don't act motivated to get out. And every time I try to bring you along in the process, you find one excuse after another not to participate." He tried to speak, but she wagged her finger. "Don't even start with the witch war. I know how serious it is. But that's only come up in the last couple days. This has been going on for months."

Max stuck a fry in his mouth. Normally at this point in their relationship cycle, Max would come to the conclusion that Sandra was right. He would see the flaw in his own thinking that led him to this point, and he would laugh at himself. They would talk a little further, he would kiss her, she would kiss him, and all the kissing would lead to some amorous fire that would relax them both and recalibrate their marriage — put them back on the right track. But this time, Sandra was not right. Max thought over his behavior, his emotions, his reasoning — it did not add up the way she suggested.

He wanted to get out of that apartment. He wanted to get a house and start a life with the Sandwich Boys in their care. He meant every word he had said to her previously — that he wanted all of those things and that he wanted to do them right. If it meant another few months going crazy in his mother's apartment, then in the long run, he believed it was worthwhile. If anything, Sandra was the one not willing to push through together. She wanted to sidestep the process, speed things up, even if it meant getting things wrong.

He said as much to her. She listened, stoic except for taking the time to eat. As he went on, she looked out the window and tapped that ruby ring against the glass.

That's when it hit him.

"You know," he said, choosing his words like a soldier stepping through a minefield. "I have always respected that you don't like to talk about your family. I've never pushed to meet them, never insisted you invite them to events in our life, nothing. But the way you've been going on about my mother, about the house, even about the Sandwich Boys — and especially with the way you've acted with that ring — it's obvious that something deeper is going on. Normally, I'd let that part of your life remain private. I'm not foolish enough to think that just because we're married means I have to know every last detail of you. But since this is touching my life, and it's going to start touching PB and J's lives as well, I think I have right to know."

As his words hung in the air, the sweet odor of the wine mixed with the greasy aroma of the burgers and fries, and the bizarre blend threatened to turn Max's stomach. But, of course, he knew better. The smell sickened him only because Sandra's continued silence shifted the earth beneath him. The car felt like it spun slowly, perceptible only out of the corner of his eye, yet if he closed his eyes, everything would spin faster. Perhaps he had drunk more wine than he realized.

As his thoughts threatened to spiral, Sandra finally said, "Your detective instincts are getting better and better." She reached over and took his hand. It was warm and smooth. He forgot how wonderful it felt to entwine his fingers with hers.

She opened her free hand in front of her face and stared at the ruby ring. In the dark of the car, it looked like a legless beetle — all dark shell. When she let her hand drop into her lap, Max swore he heard a hard click like something striking that shell. Sandra sniffled.

With a shaking breath, she said, "I grew up with an unreliable family. I've told you about my father — that he wasn't really there. But it was more like he was there, then he was gone, then he was there, then he was gone. I never knew when to expect him to be around because there was never any regularity to any of it."

"And your mother drank, right?"

She nodded. "I don't want you to get the wrong idea. I was never abused or messed with. Not physically anyway. Mostly, I felt like a piece of furniture."

"This is all the stuff you told me since we first started getting serious."

"Give me a chance to warm up to this. It's not easy for me."

Not wanting to make things more uncomfortable, Max stayed silent. He took a bite of his burger for something to do.

Sandra closed her eyes and sighed. When she opened them, her gaze drifted into the years past. "I know I've told you a little about my parents before, but it's only been in broad strokes. And the big thing that happened in my life back then, also something I've told you about, was my brother's accident. He was a teenager in a car with a bunch of other teenagers and they had been drinking. Before that, my mother drank for two reasons — she was miserable with the way my father treated us and she wanted to quiet the things she saw. The ghosts. At least, that's what I think — I had to get my ability to see ghosts from somewhere."

"You've told me she —"

"I know. And all of that was true. But there was another truth. That's what it's like living in my kind of family. There's a surface layer of the family, and then there are all these other shadowy layers underneath. It's part of why I don't like talking about them. It's very confusing and hard to explain. And after Cameron came back from the hospital, it only got worse. He needed constant care. Even after he could take care of himself, he needed therapy and medicine and the cost was crazy. The family fell apart. My father would disappear for longer periods of time, and my mother would be sober for less. I started having to take care of myself. It was more of those layers. I'd go to school. I'd join sports and activities and acted like a normal kid. But then I'd go home, and I would have to be my own parent. A family of one living with these other people who may have been their own family. I don't know."

She kept a tight grip on Max's hand, and he took that as a good sign. She grew still for a moment. The shushing of cars drifting by met with a soft patter of rain drops against the roof of the car. Max hadn't noticed when the rain began, but puddles had already formed in the parking lot.

"My mother lost her job." Sandra gazed down at the ruby ring. "I don't know how she found the money to drink more and more, but she did. I don't like to think about that too often. Eventually, my father stopped showing up at all. I was old enough to know that things were looking bad but not old enough to know what to do about it. I didn't tell anybody. The teachers and the administration — they were the enemy. All they were going to do was call social services. Looking back, that might not have been a bad thing, but at the time, no way. Not for me.

"So, I started pawning things. Little by little, everything in the house started getting sold. I'd hide the money so that my mom wouldn't use it for more booze. A few times, we got a letter from my dad with a check inside. I'd forge my mom's signature and that would keep us going for a while. My brother wasted away right next to her. They were both miserable, but at least they had each other. I had nobody. By the time I graduated high school and managed to snag a few scholarships and loans for college, there was nothing left to pawn. Except this ring.

"Last time I saw my mom, she was passed out on the couch as I left for freshman orientation. I kept the ring, obviously. It's been in my mess of a jewelry box for years. I never wanted to look at it, never wanted to get rid of it, never wanted to wear it."

"Until now."

"Part of the reason I didn't want kids was that I didn't want to do any of this kind of crap to them. It's not right to give a kid a strong family and then cut it out from underneath."

"But you're the one who pushed to become the Sandwich Boys' guardians."

"With the boys, I see it different. I figure anything we offer them is a huge step up from the streets. But now —"

Max saw the shimmering in her eyes, and his chest tightened. "Honey, we are not your parents. We're not my parents, either. You thinking about these things means that you won't make the same mistakes. You're aware of them, and you're actively working against being like that."

"I know. I do. At least, I know it in my head." She patted her chest. "But here — it's a lot harder to believe."

Taking both her hands in his, Max said, "That is why you have me. That's why being married means we do these things together."

Wiping her fingers under her eyes, she sniffed. "Now you know. I should have told you a long time ago. I'm sorry." She shuddered. "I don't want to start thinking about it all over again. You talk now. You have a side to this, too. Why don't you tell me about how it's been for you? I'm sure your mom's driving you crazy with all of her Little Max stuff."

Max grunted. "It's not too bad."

Sandra shoved his shoulder and laughed. "I see the way you cringe every time she starts in. *Oh, when Max was little, oh little Max, oh, oh, oh.*"

Max joined in the laughter. "I'll tell you this — I won't

miss any of that at all once we move out."

"What else?"

"Other than not hearing my mother embarrassing me? Well, I guess I just need to get laid."

They both stared at each other and broke into raucous laughter. It continued to the point of starting to hurt Max's chest as he gasped for air.

"Well," Sandra said, at length, "come on over here, big boy. Momma wants some action to."

"No, no. Don't ever do that *Momma* stuff."

"What? Would you prefer Little Max?"

"Are you trying to kill the mood?"

Before Sandra could come up with another ridiculous name, Max pressed his mouth against hers. She giggled as she kissed him back. It had been ages since they made out in the backseat of a car, and while Max would have preferred the luxury of a bed or a couch or any comfortable surface, they were not in a position to be choosy.

"Put on some music," Sandra said.

He leaned over the driver's seat and turned the key to power the car. He flipped on the radio.

"… light showers with temperatures overnight cooling to fifty-two degrees." Max reached to change the station when he heard the announcer go on, *"More details are coming in about the brutal murders of two Greensboro residents found at the O. Henry Hotel. The bodies were discovered when housekeeping crews entered a room for cleaning. They found two men, dead, tied to chairs, with most of their skin removed. According to officers on the scene, they have not come across anything like this in all their years on the force. Angie Gibbons has the latest."*

Max shut off the radio. He glanced back at Sandra, and the shock reverberating throughout his body registered on her face. The O. Henry Hotel — headquarters of the Magi.

"Shit."

Chapter 12

THE NEXT DAY, as the sun peeked out from the clouds and promised warmth and sunshine for the afternoon, Max and Sandra drove to the O. Henry Hotel. After dealing with Mrs. Porter all morning — she insisted that they should not have gone out and left her alone — Max and Sandra played out the possibilities of their future. The car ride felt longer and longer with each negative outcome they envisioned. Everything from death to being cursed eternally to being forced out of the state to losing the boys to social services. By the time they reached the hotel, they had no idea better than to keep their heads down and hope the witches destroyed each other without causing too much collateral damage. Max would have appreciated Drummond's input, but the ghost had spent the evening with his new buddy, Irene Beck, and had yet to return.

Max peered up at the hotel. A ten story box of brick and granite that he always thought looked appropriate for a boutique hotel in a New York City suburb. But here, in the middle of a Greensboro parking lot near the Friendly Shopping Center, it stood out as both odd and curious. Thankfully, the police no longer surrounded the place. Max imagined they had been there for hours with their flashing lights and repetitive questions. He wondered if any of the police had stumbled upon the hotel's biggest secret — that Mother Hope ran all of the Magi operations from private floors at the top of this building as well as several secret floors beneath.

As he and Sandra entered, Max inhaled the earthy wood

of the fireplace and enjoyed the old library feel of the lobby. Everything about the place called out its old-style elegance — from the heavy furniture to the classical music playing softly in the background to the brass elevator doors. It was a small pleasure, but he wanted every little bit he could take before all of North Carolina burned in a witch war.

They walked by the reception desk and toward the open sitting area. The ceiling stretched three stories above, and at the top, the words of O. Henry's most famous story, *The Gift of the Magi*, spiraled down in an artistic flourish. In truth, though, the words hid an incantation that protected the hotel and the Magi.

Didn't protect two of the Magi, Max thought.

They knew the routine. All visitors to the hotel were monitored by surveillance cameras and, most likely, a spell or two. If they waited around long enough, somebody would come for them. Before they reached an overstuffed sofa, however, a large woman with close-cropped hair approached. "You Mr. and Mrs. Porter?"

Max nodded. She motioned with her head the way all bodyguards and bouncers seem to do — an implied demand to be followed. As they set off behind the woman's lead, Max wondered if there was a special school that taught the move.

"I haven't seen you around here before," he said. "You new? Or just new to this particular part of the job?"

The woman did not answer.

"Only reason I'm asking is because we're regulars when it comes to visiting Mother Hope. I figure if I'm going to be bumping into you a lot, it might be nice to know your name, at the least."

The woman stopped. She turned her head back. "Annie." She headed off again.

She led them to an elevator bank that Max had never seen before. They waited to the soft yet haunting sounds of one of Chopin's nocturnes. Max opened his mouth to engage with Annie some more, but Sandra poked him in the side. He held back and listened to the gentle music.

They rode up to the top floor, and Annie led them to the end of the hall. A man slightly larger than Annie stood at the door. He wore a black suit, black tie, and had a bulge under his arm. Max put out his arms, expecting to be frisked.

The man shifted closer as if imparting a secret. "No need, Mr. Porter. I know you can't do anything to her without getting yourself hurt. Go on in."

Without intending to do so, Max rubbed the area of his chest where Mother Hope had cursed him. The man opened the door, and Max and Sandra walked in. Annie whispered something to the man before following behind them.

Max had been in Mother Hope's apartment before. It amazed him how modern and sterile the place looked. Mostly white, hard furniture that had a plastic appearance though he imagined it was actually some expensive material. The place reminded him of what filmmakers in the 60s thought the future might be like. But rather than a hopeful, utopian sensation, the room left Max more aware than ever of the darkness underneath. Mother Hope could be cruel, vindictive, and powerfully vicious. No amount of artistic furniture could fool him into thinking otherwise.

"This way," Annie said, guiding them toward the back.

With her colossal footsteps bumping the ground, Annie brought Max and Sandra down a narrow corridor that ended with a glass door. She slid open the door and stood aside, gesturing for them to enter.

They stepped into a garden that should not have been.

They were not on the roof, there was no skylight, yet a lush utopia spread out before them. Magic, of course. Magic had caused the sunlight. Magic had transformed a basic hotel room into a garden paradise. Magic had cut the supports from under reality.

Trees from all over the world reached impossibly high. A kaleidoscope of flowers perfumed the air. Two yellow swallowtails fluttered by while somewhere hidden in the canopy above, birds played out their musical call and response.

Max could not tell which parts were illusions and which parts were real. He guessed that was the intention. Sandra's awed gasp reminded him how much her appreciation of magic had grown with her studies. Even when that magic came from the hands of a witch like Mother Hope, Sandra still found it within herself to be impressed.

They strolled down a short path that opened into a wide, precise circle surrounded by stones. In the middle, sitting cross-legged on a wooden platform, Mother Hope meditated. It was Max's turn for an awed gasp.

The old woman's eyes fluttered open. She lifted her head, the jangling of her coin-lined scarf blended with the birds singing above. She often dressed like an old gypsy out of the movies, but the costume did not look outlandish on her. If anything, Max found her more intimidating.

"Really, Mr. Porter, meditation is very good for centering oneself. And especially good for a witch." She arched her head to focus on Sandra. "Especially if you want to perform difficult or complex spells. Meditation is often the overlooked ingredient."

"I'll remember that," Sandra said.

Max stepped forward. "I apologize for disturbing your centering then. We only came here to pay our respects. We heard last night on the radio about the deaths."

Mother Hope set her feet on the ground and groaned as she stood. A bit shorter than Max's mother, Mother Hope intimidated him far worse. "Pay respects. Like you did for the Mobleys?"

Hoping he did not hesitate, he said, "That shouldn't surprise you. We worked for them once before. It was the decent thing to do."

"You work for me."

"And I won't forget it."

She ambled close to Max and tapped his chest — the exact spot of the curse. "I know you won't."

"I thought I was doing a good thing for the Magi. Since your mission is to quell magic, to make sure it does not get abused, then it seemed to me that having good relations with one of the most powerful covens in the area was a smart approach."

Puffing up her cheeks, she acted as if she gave his word serious consideration. But Max knew it was an act. "You are intelligent enough to know that it was the Mobley coven who flayed two of our people," she said. "Do those seem like the kinds of witches we want to befriend?"

"Perhaps they were retaliating against who they thought had killed two of their own. Of course, I'm sure you were not responsible. After all, though heated at times, things between these two groups had seemed to reach a bit of a stasis. Why would you want to go ruin that?"

"Careful, Mr. Porter. Never trust a witch. When things seem stable and at peace, that is when they are most dangerous. The Mobley coven has always been about power. They use witchcraft as a method to manipulate people in an effort to gain power — over people's lives, over control of land, even as a way to influence our government. They are evil, deadly women."

"Yet you've never made a move against them before."

With a knowing grin, Mother Hope said, "Don't try to verbally spar with me. You'll always lose. You're far better at smartass comments then thoughtful slights." With two fingers gently pressing against his chest, she pushed Max to the side. Stepping closer to Sandra, she said, "I've had my eye on you. You've become quite skilled at witchcraft."

Reddening, Sandra nodded. "Thank you."

"There are rough times ahead. You and your husband spend your days investigating ghosts and fighting witches, and as I've often told him, that's exactly the sort of work the Magi group is all about. We make a good team together. We can, anyway. Perhaps you will be the more sensible of your agency. Whenever you're ready, you only need to come here. I can teach you so much."

"Thank you for your time," Max said, rushing to Sandra's side. "Like I said, we came to pay our respects. We're sorry for your loss. We'll be on our way now."

Escorting Sandra out of the garden, he could feel the old woman's eyes burning through his back. With one side blatantly acknowledging a war, and now this other side being coy about what was obvious, Max suspected matters would only get worse. But he knew he had to take it one step further.

Pausing to turn back, he said, "Quick question, here. Do you know anything about a man named Wilburn Walker? Or perhaps William Crutchfield?"

He saw the recognition on her face. He couldn't tell if he was surprised or not, but deep down, he had expected as much.

"I've been alive a long time," she said, her words pleasantly covering up all the dark malice he saw flashing in her eyes. "I've met a lot of people. I think perhaps the names sound familiar, but I'd have to give it some time to remember."

"No problem. Just a thought. Again, our condolences."

As before, Annie provided an escort to the elevator. But this time, she did not ride with them. Once Max and Sandra boarded the elevator, Annie leaned in, pressed the lobby button and let the door close on them alone.

Taking Max's hand, Sandra said, "I guess that could have gone worse."

"Definitely. After all, I'm still alive."

Neither of them managed even a chuckle.

As if the day could not get weirder, when the elevator doors opened, an old, familiar face greeted them — Leon Moore.

"I warned you this was coming," Leon said. "You need to follow me so we can talk."

Chapter 13

LEON DID NOT LOOK as good as he had in the past. When he had joined with the Magi and became Mother Hope's right hand, she gifted him by reducing the ravages of age. The day Max had first met him at the Z. Smith Reynolds Library, Leon was a black man with white hair around a mostly bald head, stooped, wrinkly, and weak. But over the years, he had grown younger and younger. Stronger and stronger. Now, however, it looked as if he had fallen out of favor with Mother Hope.

While Max and Sandra stared dumbfounded at the old man, Leon did not wait for a reply. He walked out of the lobby and into the parking lot. For an old man, he moved surprisingly well. He crossed the parking lot, reached a crosswalk, and went over into the shopping center.

Max and Sandra followed behind, never stopping him, never asking him for an answer. They both had been through enough to know that following and keeping quiet would be the best play for the moment. At length, he turned down toward the big department stores, cut into a small alcove of smaller stores, and entered a deli.

The place had a used look to it — dirty and chipped floor tiles, a long L-shaped counter with torn seat covers on the stools, and stains on the walls from sources Max wanted to know nothing about. Considering the rents for such a prime location, Max wondered how they could stay in business. Unless they were laundering money for organized crime. Or for the Magi.

He checked the faces of those behind the counter once

more. The handful of customers also favored a quick look. He did not recognize any of them from his previous visits to the O. Henry Hotel.

As Max and Sandra joined Leon at a booth, Max said, "It's a little early for lunch, but I guess I can eat."

Leon shoved the menu across the table. "Eat, don't eat. I don't care. I just need to be a little bit away from the prying eyes of the Magi."

"And a deli a few blocks away is far enough?"

"I can't be choosy right now, and I can't be gone for too long. A lot's happening and I got to keep on it all at once."

With a gentle tone, Sandra said, "Please, tell us what's got you so upset."

"Are you kidding?"

"I meant specifics. Obviously losing two members of your group in such a brutal way —"

"I don't care about them. They were a couple of weasels who wanted to get in on Mother Hope's good side and then skim from her in one way or another. I'm worried about the bigger picture. The war that's coming."

Max said, "Based on the last two days, I'd say the war is already here."

A waitress walked over but Leon waved her away. "You're right about that. I told you the last time we met that Mother Hope was acting strange. I warned you something serious was coming down the line, and here we are."

"If this is just going to be a lot of *I told you so,* then we've got better things to do."

Leon's face dropped in incredulous shock. "Blood's been spilled. We have to prepare."

"*We?* We don't have anything to do with you."

"You're part of the Magi whether you want to be or not."

Sandra said, "Just because Max was cursed by Mother Hope doesn't make him part of the Magi."

"It does mean he's got to listen to what she says. Because if you don't, she'll flip the switch on that curse — and since the two of you decided to be as evil as the witches and link your curse to me, that means she would be flipping the switch on me, too. That's one of many things got me worried."

There were several ways to approach this, and having spent time learning from Drummond, Max recognized a few. He could take on the role of the hard ass — threaten Leon to spy for him and try to control Mother Hope through that knowledge, but Max had too much to juggle already. He did not need to add more headaches to the chaos in his life. Another option — force Leon to join the whole gang at the Porter Agency. Except they could never trust the man. He would more than likely be a spy for Mother Hope than an asset for Max. A far easier choice — play it straight up the middle by seeing if his suspicions about everybody's connection to the case panned out.

"What can you tell me about Wilburn Walker?" Max asked.

"Never heard of him."

For the first time, Max actually believed that response. "What about Henry or Mary Goins?"

"No. Who are these people? What do they have to do with any of this?"

Sandra tapped the laminated table with her fingertip. "You better stop stonewalling us. You're all worried that Mother Hope might flick Max's switch and hurt you in the process — don't forget we can hurt you, too."

Leon gripped the table and lowered his head. "I'm telling you the truth. I don't know those people."

"But you know something," Max said. "You may not be

Mother Hope's favorite at the moment, but she didn't toss you aside either. What is she having you do?"

Leon rubbed his forehead as if suffering a migraine. His hand then lowered over the stubble on his face and he gazed out the window. "You know, when I first met you, I thought *There is a man after my own heart.* I always loved the library, the research, the digging into history and discovering things that nobody else had found. Not because they were hard-to-find or some amazing kind of revelation, though sometimes that happened, but simply because nobody took the time, nobody had the patience and determination, nobody had the audacity to just sit down and do the work." Bringing his hands together as if in prayer, he then pointed toward Max. "But you — you've always been willing to do whatever is necessary to find the smallest scrap of information, the tiniest hint of a fragment of a clue to whatever subject you're investigating. I really liked that about you."

"I liked it when you were simply a librarian trying to help me out. All of this crap — I really wish we weren't sitting on opposite sides of a table."

"Except, I suppose I always was opposite you. Mother Hope had her claws into me before I met you. The Magi — the idea of the Magi is what appeals to me. The things they say they stand for."

"People get complacent. They start to think an institution will run itself and that it will always run properly. That's how corruption takes root. All the people who put the thing together are no longer around and others come along with greed in their hearts."

Sandra reached across the table and took Leon's hand. "Bad things are coming our way — for all of us. You know that. Yesterday, the Mobleys made a point of letting us know they could reach our sons. This war is going to overflow way beyond just the witches and the Magi. Regular people are going to get hurt. Please, please help us. Tell us something that we can use."

Leon placed his hand atop hers, and as if agreeing to give up the last thing he ever valued, his body drooped. "Mother Hope asked me to search for the grave of a man named William Crutchfield. She's got me inspecting every cemetery in the state. I figured it was busy work, but looking at your faces, it seems that name may mean something."

Max said, "It does."

"Do you know who this guy was? Where I can find his resting place?"

"I'm looking for him too. If you find his grave, please text me the address."

"You do the same for me."

For a few seconds, all three exchanged looks without a word being spoken. With an abrupt motion, Leon slid out of the booth. He paused as if about to say something, then thought better of it. He finally rested his hand on Sandra's shoulder and closed his eyes. It seemed to Max that the man prayed. Then he strolled out of the restaurant.

"That was weird," Sandra said.

Max set the menu aside. "Time to go back. I got a ghost to find."

Chapter 14

THE REST OF THE AFTERNOON, Max worked at his mother's apartment. Sandra needed to research the symbol from the cloaked witch's casting circle, and the best way for her to do that was to use the casting circle in the office. In order to give her a peaceful place to concentrate, Max opted to go home. He considered a visit to the library, but with all that had happened to J, he thought the boy might appreciate seeing Max's face when he got home from school. J certainly looked unhappy about going back to school that morning.

Sitting on the long couch, Max propped his laptop against his knees and continued taking notes on William Crutchfield. Off to his right, by the window, PB worked on multiplication and division of fractions while Max's mother watched over the boy's shoulder. Now and then, she made small noises — some approving, some warning of a pending mistake. PB focused on his work, and in a strange way, the two appeared happy with their roles — strange because most teenage boys would be rebelling against any authority figure. But each time Mrs. Porter gave the boy structure, he thrived.

The same could not be said for William Crutchfield. What small amount Max could find on the man suggested he had a healthy distaste for things like law and order. Yet Walker had been telling the truth — a man named William Crutchfield did turn up at the Bakersville, California Sheriff's Department in 1904 and claimed to have been involved with the murders from so many years before in

North Carolina. The first thing that stood out to Max suggesting that this man might actually be Straw Hat lay in the alias.

Back in 1891, when the Winston police were heavily involved in charging people for the murders of Mary Goins and John Smith, three men had been arrested in connection to the crime. Lack of evidence set all three men free. They were Owen Walker, William Fansler, and Charles Crutchfield. The odds that this man in California happened to share the first name of William Fansler and the last name of Charles Crutchfield seemed highly unlikely.

Once Max decided that William Crutchfield was, in all likelihood, Straw Hat, following the man's movements became easier. Whatever his reasoning, Crutchfield retained the alias. Max kept expecting the trail to go cold, but it led right back to Winston.

"Very good," Mrs. Porter said. "You know, when Max was little, when he was my Little Max, he struggled with fractions. He did. All through school. I tried to help him like I'm helping you, but he would fight it and cry and whine and complain. You are a much better student than he ever was."

PB had the sense not to say anything, but he could not hide the pride glowing off of him. Max gave him a thumbs up, and the boy went back to work on the next problem.

Max located a manifest that listed William Crutchfield as a passenger aboard the SS North Dakota. About a decade too early for use of the Panama Canal, he had to take the long way, going down the Peruvian coast, around Argentina's Cape Horn, and back up along Brazil. Upon arriving in North Carolina, he apparently returned to his old stomping ground. In fact, according to the diary of Victoria Brandymore, old Straw Hat may have had vengeance on his mind.

August 24, 1905
It was so good to spend time with my old friend. He asks
that we call him Crutchfield now, and we all agreed to
do so. Just another one of his eccentricities. His travels
have suited him well. He looks healthy and strong and
handsome as ever. I do hope he'll spend more time with
me once his business affairs are concluded. The only
downside to the evening was his constant mentioning of
women that I did not know. I had come fully prepared to
help him find old W——, but he seemed more worried
about these old flames. What's a girl to do? Maybe
Edna was right. I should just let the wild ones go and
put my heart into a more stable man like Samuel or
Reginald.

Max wondered if one of those women went by the name
Mobley. Or possibly even Mother Hope. If vengeance
wasn't his goal — and according to the diary entry, he
showed a lack of interest in Wilburn Walker (if, indeed,
W—— was Walker) — then maybe his fascination with
witchcraft had sent him down the wrong road.

He read what more of the diary existed, about twenty
pages, but beyond that entry, Ms. Brandymore had nothing
to say of value. She did reference the fact that she knew
Crutchfield by another name, but whatever that name was,
it most likely was another alias. Still, Max made a note to
check it out in case he hit a dead end.

"You did it again," Mrs. Porter said. "Perfect. Little
Max, you better watch out. PB here is going to be able to
do all the accounting for your company soon."

Max said, "That would be wonderful. I hate doing the
paperwork."

Slapping his laptop shut, he rolled up to his feet and

headed to the front door. He needed some quiet to think through all the details he had discovered, and that kind of quiet would not be found in the cramped quarters of the apartment.

"Oh, don't be like that," Mrs. Porter said. "We're only teasing."

Max made a show of stretching his back. "It's fine. I'm just going to get a little air. I've been sitting for far too long." He took the stairwell down to the front entrance, stepped outside, and inhaled the cool, evening air. Pieces were coming together. He didn't know how it all made sense yet, but his research intuition told him he neared a solution.

"About time," Drummond said, appearing in front of Max. "I've been waiting over two hours for you."

"You could've come inside at any time."

"Why would I want to do that? After all the complaining I hear between you and your wife about your mother's place, the last thing I want to do is go in there unless I had to."

Not wanting to get drawn into discussions of his mother, Max asked Drummond the key question. "Did you find William Crutchfield?"

The ghost shook his head. "He's not in the Other, either. Maybe the cemeteries are the place to go. That's where we found Walker."

Max took a few minutes to outline what he had learned about Crutchfield. When he mentioned that Crutchfield might have taken a ship around Cape Horn, Drummond made a face.

"What?" Max said.

"Travel back in those days wasn't the best thing for a person. Especially travel that isolated you in a confined space for a lengthy period of time."

"If you're thinking he got sick and died, you'd be mistaken. The diary entry I found on the Historical Society website says otherwise. He definitely made it back to North Carolina."

"That doesn't mean he didn't get sick later. And if he was, in fact, involved with one of the witches, that sickness may not have been natural."

"Hmm." Max brought out his phone and pulled up the Historical Society site again. After flicking around for a minute, he said, "I wonder ..."

"You going to keep standing there making noises or you going to let me in on whatever it is you're thinking?"

Looking up, Max reddened. "Sorry. It's just that I remembered a few references to something called a *pest house*."

"Oh, sure."

"You know what that is?"

"Back in my day, and long before my day, pest houses were places to quarantine people. They were houses usually on the edge of town or further away. Somebody comes down with a disease that's highly contagious, and you send them to the pest house. I never actually saw one, thankfully. They were not known as pleasant places. And, frankly, if you ended up going to one, your chances of ever getting out alive were slim. You think Crutchfield went to one of these places?"

"Seems like a possibility. Especially because he took a ship all the way from California to here. Like you said, possibility of picking up a disease on his way, especially going around South America, it's not that hard to believe. Except this lady, Victoria Brandymore — she wrote in her diary that she saw him and said he looked healthy."

Drummond crossed his arms and thought. "Smallpox. He could have been infected over a week and not known."

Bouncing from one foot to the other, Max said, "Yeah. This connects. I can see it."

"You got that bookworm excitement I've seen before. Does this mean you're headed off to cram your head in a bunch of texts?"

"If Crutchfield was sick with smallpox or some other horrible disease, he would have ended up in a pest house. There can't be that many of them around because if there were, I would've heard about them long before now."

"Modern medicine did away with them."

"And it's not like somebody would come along and want to live in a house like that. They'd have been tough to sell. There can't be that many still standing or they'd be more well-known. So, if one is still around, it might be a historical landmark. I can search for that easy. All we have to do is figure out which one Crutchfield went to, and chances are —"

"We'll find Crutchfield."

"Okay, I've got to go back inside and do some research on my laptop. You're welcome to hang out in the apartment."

"Gee, that sounds like such a swell time. I think I'll float around out here for a while. When you're ready, come on out and call for me."

Back in the apartment, Max delved into research on pest houses and his attempt to locate any still standing in North Carolina. As he worked, part of his brain noted J returning from school and both boys helping Mrs. Porter prepare dinner. Shortly after, Sandra came home.

She dropped on the couch close to Max so they could discuss things without being overheard. "I tried out a lot of what I know," she said. "Not much luck. It's a very old symbol, and a rather unorthodox version of it. That's the problem. The classic version of it would be some kind of location spell, but the drawing was very strange. One of those kinds of things that makes you think the person drawing it is either insane or a genius."

"A location spell would make sense — trying to find Wilburn Walker since he was the last known connection to Crutchfield."

"Only problem is the symbol could also be some kind of curse or maybe a different kind of attack. None of the books I have go back far enough to match it exactly. I put out a couple calls, but this late in the day, nobody's going to bother calling me back."

"Really? I'd think witches didn't even get started on their day until the sun went down."

"And you think they're eager to do busywork for me? Besides, with everything that's going on, most witches don't want to talk to me at all. They don't want to be seen as taking sides with us."

"So, tomorrow?"

"If I'm lucky. Otherwise, I'll have to figure out some way to get access to a few fairly rare books."

Max looked at the boys and Mrs. Porter in the kitchen before turning his attention back on his wife. His gut told him one thing while his chest told him another. He could see that she had noticed the turmoil on his face, but she simply waited for him to speak.

"I've got a hunch where I can find Crutchfield."

"That's good, isn't it?"

"Yeah, but it bothers me that the witches in the area are getting cold feet. If they won't talk to you about something as simple as that symbol, things are even worse than I realized. And I realized a lot."

Max smelled the onions and green peppers sautéing on the stove. They sizzled and crackled, and the boys jumped back as a small bubble of oil popped. With nervous laughter, they edged back in as Mrs. Porter stirred the pan.

Watching them, Max said, "I know you're not going to like this, but I was wondering if you would take the boys and my mother out of state? Just for a few days. A week at most. Let this situation cool down."

"Absolutely not." No anger. No frustration. Simply matter of fact. "First off, if we even tried to leave the state, the witches would know. Mother Hope and Grandma Mobley are not fools. They'd find out and they would never allow it. Secondly, and far more important, we are a team. You need me."

He had no expectation of a different outcome, but he held a glimmer of hope. In his mind, he had leapt ahead to what seemed the logical culmination of all the paths converging. He did not like what he saw.

"Okay," he said, placing his hand on her knee. "At least, watch the boys the rest of the night. I've got to get out of here. Finish my research in quiet."

"Of course." She picked up his hand and kissed his palm. "See? You do need me."

He chuckled.

"You know what else you need? Your own home. If you had your own place, your own study once more, none of this would be a problem."

The smile on his face dropped. "How could you bring that up right now? We've talked through this, and —"

"Exactly for that reason. We did talk through this. And you keep missing the point. You ask me to take the boys and leave? The point is that we do this stuff together. You've always known it, and every time you get scared, you forget. So I'm here to remind you. Witches or no witches, life goes on. And our life would run much smoother with our own roof over our heads." She kissed his palm again. "I'm not trying to make you feel guilty. Not trying to pressure you. I just want you to see the bigger picture."

He looked into her eyes and saw her sincerity. He gazed back at the boys once more. "I do see it. And I love you, too."

As Max headed to his car, he scanned the parking lot. Too many times he had been attacked by focusing on getting his key in the door rather than being aware of his surroundings. Never again.

Despite his attempted awareness, Drummond managed to sneak up behind him. "Ready to get the work?"

Max jumped and tried to pass it off with a laugh. Getting into his car, he said, "I have a hunch how we can find Crutchfield. The answer is in the branch office of the North Carolina Historical Society."

Drummond made a face as if he smelled something foul. "That's as bad as spending time with you in a library."

"Trust me, you'll have fun."

"I highly doubt that."

"The sun's gone down. The building is most likely closed. That means you're going to help me break in."

Perking up, Drummond said, "A break in? That's more like it."

Chapter 15

THOUGH THE HISTORICAL SOCIETY'S BRANCH OFFICE was technically a state building, Max did not expect it to be highly secure. Located off Broad Street, Max parked three blocks away to be safe. Just because his expectations were for an easy break-in, he did not want to take chances.

Walking toward the converted townhouse, Max avoided conversation with Drummond — he did not want to draw attention from anybody passing by. Drummond seemed to understand, or at least, he was in a quiet mood. Either way, they did not discuss anything until they reached the building.

The branch office stood three stories with a brick front and white-trimmed windows. From the outside, the place looked sturdy despite its age. Except the closer they came, the more Max saw that the brick was only a layer of siding. Not real at all. In fact, the house had been constructed like any other wood frame dwelling. Only the surrounding buildings protected this place from high winds and storms.

Drummond slipped through the faux-brick walls, rummaged around for a bit, and returned. "Looks clear. Just a basic locked door."

"Can you unlock it from the inside?"

"I think so. I didn't see a keypad or any kind of surveillance equipment. It's really just an old house."

"I figured that might be the case. The actual Historical Society headquarters is in Raleigh — that's where the majority of important papers pertaining to the state are found. We're only looking for things related to pest houses in Winston-Salem. If William Crutchfield needed such a place, he would not travel far across the state."

"Just to be safe, I think you should enter through the back door."

Max nodded and followed the ghost down a concrete alley. They emerged in a small parking area for two cars. Wooden steps led up to a patio that connected to the back door. Drummond slipped through again, and Max could see him as he checked over the door one final time. Then, wincing through the entire experience, Drummond unlocked the sliding glass door. Max slid it open and paused. He listened for any sound of an alarm and looked for any blinking lights. Nothing.

He entered and waited again — this time wondering if he would hear police sirens scream from a few blocks away. When the quiet continued, he turned on his flashlight and headed deeper inside.

The building's former glory as a residential townhouse had not been altered much — at least, not on the first floor. Several rooms had been converted into offices but the walls remained, the original flooring remained, the old doors remained. Even the kitchen in the back remained a kitchen. Max took the stairs to the second floor where the real changes had been made. The walls between bedrooms had been knocked down and replaced with a bank of file cabinets pressed up against each other. A metal desk with rusty corners occupied the middle of the room.

"There are essentially two kinds of records kept in these places — things of local interest and things nobody knows what to do with," Max said as he opened the nearest cabinet. "All the really important documents have either been digitized or are in the queue to be digitized. Those would all be in Raleigh — everything from things mentioning historical figures to newspapers and photographs of key events in our state's history. But here is where we find the Winston-Salem specifics. All the documents and papers that don't have value to the Raleigh office or haven't been donated to one of our university libraries."

"The dregs."

"As far as they all might see it, yes. But for us, this is a gold mine. I know what I want hasn't been digitized because I couldn't access it from my laptop. So, somewhere in these files there are lists of every person who ever went through a Winston-Salem pest house. Once we find those lists, I can cut through to him in no time. We find his name and we'll know where to go."

As Max rifled through cabinet after cabinet, folder after folder, page after page, Drummond stood guard. He hovered at the staircase, floated around the perimeter of the house, and kept Max apprised of anybody suspicious coming their way. He also provided Max with ample unwanted distractions.

"Are you sure Crutchfield wound up in a pest house? I don't mean to doubt your research abilities, but there are a lot of places he could have met his end. We don't even know for sure that he was sick."

"We actually have quite a lot to go on — by process of elimination. One, we know that Crutchfield is not in the Other because you checked. Two, we know that Crutchfield is not in any of the cemeteries that Walker could've been in because I checked and I would've spotted the name. Plus, Walker would have had a confrontation with Crutchfield, and I doubt he forgot to mention that fact. Three, we can assume that Crutchfield did not move on to whatever is beyond being a ghost because he was an evil man with a lot of baggage. Prime material for being screwed over in the ghost department. Now, technically speaking, you're right. It's very possible that Crutchfield never left California or never even was Straw Hat to begin with. It could all be a wild coincidence. But come on. You don't believe it and neither do I. Besides which, Grandma Mobley and Mother Hope are about to rain magic Hell down upon all of North Carolina and it seems that this guy has something to do with some of it. Add to all of that the trip around South America where it would have been easy to contract a disease, and it is a strong possibility that we're on the right track."

Max returned to the file cabinets. He hated to admit it, but he shared Drummond's doubts. He had built his conclusion upon a lot of intuitive leaps. It would not take much to collapse the unstable structure of this idea. As he pulled out a few files and set them on a nearby worktable, he hoped that his research brain would not let them down.

"For what it's worth," Drummond said, "I talked with Irene the other night about the case. She thinks you're on the right track, too. Told me that a number of years ago she worked regularly with the police. In those few cases that they brought her in, she ended up getting into the minds of some pretty sick individuals. That stopped her from doing that work ever again. But at the time, she had to live with it, and she said that this Crutchfield sounds like he fits the bill. A real sick mind that would have built up all that went down as wrongs against him. Probably blamed Walker for it all. In her opinion, he definitely came back to North Carolina. No matter the threat to his getting caught and incarcerated, he would feel compelled to return."

"Maybe. But why didn't he go after Walker right away, then?"

"If you're right, he was sick. He may have decided that he had a cold or something. Take a few days to rest, and then go after Walker."

"Only he never got well again."

"Ends up forced into a pest house, and that's that."

Max buried his thoughts in the work. Reading old handwriting on decaying pieces of paper by flashlight required a lot of his attention. Two hours of it, in fact.

He made several piles of reports that listed pest house residents. A few piles were of those well past the year of Crutchfield's supposed return. One pile was of lists Max checked and dismissed. Another pile was of lists Max checked but found names too difficult to decipher. These bore illegible handwriting with names that looked like *Kertchfd, Crutch,* and *Cuthfeld*. If Max could not find Crutchfield in any of the other documents, he would return to these for a closer inspection.

But as he opened the next folder, he found a photograph with the edges rippled and one corner coffee-stained. It depicted one of the last pest houses in Rockingham County. The house rose in the background and about a dozen adults stood in front for a portrait — men and women wearing threadbare clothes and looking as sick as they most likely felt. A white rope made a line that they were not allowed to cross. This quarantine rope gave them the freedom to walk out of the house but not get far enough to cause problems. Matching the photo with paperwork, Max smacked the table as he popped to his feet.

"Tell me we've got him," Drummond said.

Max brought out his phone and searched for the location of the house in Rockingham County. It sat right on the edge with Forsyth County — where Winston-Salem was located. There were two other pest houses he had found paperwork mentioning the area. Armed with names, he made a few, highly targeted keyword searches. Neither house existed anymore — one had become property for a private school while the other had been turned into farmland. But the Rockingham pest house still stood.

Max set his phone down and smiled. "Yeah, we got him."

Drummond brought his hands together in a proud clap. As Max returned the files and cleaned up any sign of his intrusion, Drummond swirled around the room.

"This is great news," the ghost said. "We'll go back and tell Sandra. Then, tomorrow, the two of you go check out the place. If it's okay with you, I'll go see Irene and try to get her to focus her talents on that area. She might be able to pick something up that'll help."

Max closed the last file cabinet and headed for the stairs. "We're going tonight."

"You want to go all the way back to your mom's place to pick up Sandra and come all the way back here and then keep going to Rockingham County? That seems a bit roundabout. Besides, you really want to be hitting a place like that at the witching hour?"

"We're not going back to get Sandra."

"Not a smart idea. Not only because she'll be pissed off, but going into a place like that without backup is the definition of stupid."

"Usually, I'd agree with you —"

"You hardly ever agree with me."

"— but in this case, we need to move now. If we bring this to Sandra, she's going to argue against me. Both of you are not taking this witch thing seriously enough. I can feel it to my bones — Grandma Mobley and Mother Hope are not having a periodic spat. This is going to be big. But if we can find Crutchfield, then maybe we can stop it before innocent people die. So, I'm going."

"But —"

"Besides, I do have backup. I've got you."

Chapter 16

As Max drove out to the border with Rockingham County, as the land darkened with dense wooded shadows, he bounced his knee and tapped the wheel. He had spent too much time in this car lately. He tried to remember what life had been like in his youth when he had an apartment in a city. It had only been for a summer internship, but it gave him a taste of a different way of life. The simple fact that in a city stores, restaurants, and music venues were all within a short walk made the days exciting. Even in a smaller city like Winston-Salem, each block had numerous cultural events pressing in against each other. The possibilities for discovery blossomed every sunrise.

But once a person got only a few miles out of the city, everything spread like marbles dumped across a table. Some people called Winston-Salem the twenty minute town because everything was within a twenty minute drive. Max had come to believe it. Sometimes, it seemed as if he spent more time in his car than anywhere else.

He thought about William Crutchfield and the long weeks on a ship. All the people he would have met, the places seen, the experiences had. Technology had changed a lot of the world, made it smaller, faster, easier to access. But that change came with a price. The disruptive effect of technology, the way it destabilized old experiences, had both good and bad outcomes. William Crutchfield was a perfect example. Taking a boat around the horn of South America — a slow, fascinating trip that would enrich one's life in a way that most could not afford today. But if

Crutchfield had access to modern medicine, he would never have died in a pest house. He would never have heard of a pest house. Heck, he would never have been on that boat. A short flight to North Carolina would have done fine and cost a quarter of a cruise.

Max turned onto a dirt road that wormed its way around the dark trees. The road crunched beneath his wheels as he barely touched the gas. Too fast and he would end up hitting a tree instead of curving by them. When he finally parked, the old house stood in his headlights like a ship emerging out of the depths of the sea. The ground sloped downward several feet from the road, and much of the land around the house had been cleared. Still, trees formed walls beyond that.

Dread pulsed off of the house hard enough that Max wondered if the place had been cursed by a witch. No need. The people who came here were cursed already.

He turned toward Drummond. "How many ghosts around this thing?"

Drummond appeared as shaken by the horrible feeling as Max. "Not a single one that I can see."

"There has to be."

Drummond squinted and leaned forward. "I'm sure they're somewhere, but they're not at the house."

Max wished that he had listened to Drummond. He could have gone back to the apartment, told Sandra, and waited until morning to visit this place. But then, he recalled meeting Walker at the cemetery — day or night didn't matter. These places would always haunt him. Plus, he wanted to get this over with.

According to his research, the pest house operated until the middle of World War I. The surrounding land had all been fields, but after a hundred years, trees grew as the land lay unused. Max checked back the way they had come. That sense of dread mutated into foreboding.

"Something wrong?" Drummond asked. "Besides the obvious."

Max motioned with his head toward the road. "Who's been maintaining this dirt road for so long?"

Drummond drifted ahead into Max's flashlight beam. He stared off into the road engulfed by the dark. Turning back, he said, "Somebody has to own this land. Maybe they keep the road clear."

Max played the flashlight back over the house. "Then why do they leave the place like this?"

"Appreciation of history?"

As they approached the house, the unsettling sensations strengthened. The building had a wide awning so that residents could spend time outside in the shade. Quite appreciated during the blistering summer months. While the house took up a sizable chunk of land, it also looked rather squat — maybe only one-and-a-half floors tall. The roof had a sharp slant. Though difficult to tell in the dark, Max suspected the roof had been made of tin. Probably rusted out by now. Rainstorms would have ruined the interior.

When they reached the front door, Max noticed how warped all the wood had become. Not just the door but the frame, walls, and the awning. One hundred years had not been kind to this house.

He pushed on the front door but it would not budge. Putting his shoulder into it, he managed to shove it back halfway. A harsh sound screeched from the old hinges.

"You're feeling gutsy," Drummond said. "Usually, you want me to go in and check out a place before you walk inside."

"Oh, yeah. I forgot about that. Well, why don't you go check out upstairs? I'll look around down here."

Max walked throughout the first floor and found it to be a spacious layout — an open plan in the modern vernacular. Back in its day, it probably proved efficient and functional. Especially if they had a lot of residents at any one time. On the far right wall, he saw a stone fireplace, and in the corner, the blackened area where a cast iron wood-burning stove had once been. A wooden bench lined the wall to the right of the fireplace.

A squeak. The bright eyes of rats glinted in his flashlight beam before scurrying into the walls. Crushed beer cans and dried-out condoms littered the corners. Clearly, teenage partiers had found this place at some point. However, it did not look as if anybody had been here recently. At least, not anybody innocent like a teenager.

The walls still gave off a negative feeling as if horrible things had happened in these rooms. Of course, they had — people had suffered and died in the house. But it felt like more than that. It felt like blood on the walls. It felt like evil.

"Max," Drummond called, and Max fumbled his flashlight. Thankfully, he caught it before it made a loud clatter on the floor. He did not want Drummond knowing how nervous he felt.

Drummond called again and Max followed the voice toward a small room in the back. Shelves lined most of the walls and a few still had rusting cans waiting to be opened. A walk-in pantry. In the far corner, a wooden ladder had been built against the wall heading straight upward to the second floor.

Drummond's head poked down. "You'll want to see this. Actually, you don't want to see it, but you're going to want to see it."

Max said, "Was that supposed to make sense?"

"Just get up here."

Max climbed the ladder slowly, testing each slat-rung before putting his full weight on it. Only one wobbled questionably. He skipped that and the rest held him fine. When he reached the top, he found a second floor that was in actuality, an attic covering the entire house. The steep roof and the lack of a full-sized second floor meant Max had to stoop or bump his head on the rafters.

Two rows had been delineated by hooks nailed into the rafters on either side of a wide section in the middle. Though empty now, Max had no trouble picturing the cots set up in each section, the dying bodies in each cot.

Drummond said, "You could probably fit twenty, maybe thirty people in here."

"Plus those downstairs."

"It gets worse. Look here."

At the head of the room, underneath a circular window, Drummond pointed to a casting circle painted into the floor. Just outside the circle, several candles had been lined up — each a different color, each at a different stage of use. Next to the red candle on the end, two severed bird claws waited to be utilized in a spell.

Drummond said, "How old you think that is? I mean, do you think that was around when the people were quarantined here, or maybe witches were using this place after it was abandoned?"

Max ran his finger along the circle, creating a trench in the dust. "It's definitely old. The paint is flaked away in places. But I find it hard to believe that this was here when the pest house was being used for its original purpose. Too many different types of people would come through. Somebody would've been morally outraged if not religiously terrified by the existence of witchcraft. And witches are very sensitive about getting found out."

"Being burned at the stake for centuries makes you a

little cautious."

"That's my point. The witches using this place would have waited until after the house became a lesser-known location."

"You're forgetting that Crutchfield had taken an interest in witchcraft. Maybe he drew this."

Max gazed up at Drummond, but before he could answer, a car door slammed shut outside.

"Stay here," Drummond said and dropped to the floor.

Max pushed up on his toes in an attempt to peek out the circular window. He could only see over the lip of the window, and from that angle, he saw trees and the full moon casting its pale blue light. Whoever owned the property must have seen a car driving off the main road and came by to investigate. Or perhaps the owner regularly visited the land to break up the parties. Or perhaps —

Drummond erupted through the floor. "I hate to say this, but it's Mother Hope and Leon."

Max stumbled back. His stomach dived low while his chest filled with a shaking bag of needles. He couldn't think straight — which might have explained his next words. "Are you sure?"

"You think there's another hundred-year-old gypsy driving around with a seventy-year-old former librarian?"

As Max's thoughts struggled to catch up to events, Mother Hope's crackling voice called out. "Don't make me wait. I'm sure your ghost has told you I'm here. Come on out. We have to talk."

Max tried to move, but his feet had become solid blocks of fright rooting into the floor. Looking at Drummond, Max simply shook his head. The rusty hinges whined downstairs as Leon and Mother Hope entered the house. The sound died in the deep woods. In the dark. In the loneliness.

What had he been thinking? Why didn't he listen to Drummond back at the Society branch office? He knew the right thing to do — go back to the apartment, tell Sandra everything, make a plan together. Was he trying to be the hero?

"You up there?" Leon asked. "I think he's up there." As Mother Hope's light steps on the wooden ladder were followed by Leon's heavy thuds, Max stared at the opening in the floor. Soon her head would rise like a shark fin lifting out of the water.

"Don't worry," Drummond said. "I'm right here with you. You've just got to snap out of it. Wake up and get that brain thinking again. You've outwitted this woman many times. You can do it again."

That was true. Mother Hope always unnerved him, but Max knew better than to let his fear take over. Perhaps the horrible things that had happened in this house left some kind of residual energy that affected his nerves. Perhaps he needed to fight harder at controlling himself. Perhaps —

"Well, well. Mr. Max Porter." Mother Hope shuffled down the middle of the attic with Leon following behind. "I always knew that we would end up like this. Someday. Always knew."

"Not really a shocker," Max said, feeling a lift in his heart at the return of his sarcasm.

"I suppose not. From the start, you never really wanted to help us out. You've had a soft spot for some witches. You've tried to suggest that some were good."

"You're a witch, and you consider yourself good."

"I use magic but I am no witch. I merely fight fire with fire. No matter. We are here now and I think you know the seriousness of the situation."

Drummond coasted closer towards Max. "It's just the two of them. I checked all around. Nobody else is here."

"How did you find me?" Max asked.

Mother Hope gestured at Leon. "Your linking curse on him works both ways. Links him to you and you to him. Makes it very easy to track you." Her eyes widened and her whole face brightened. "Look at you. So surprised. Did you really think you could outsmart me? Ha. I've known for a long time that you cursed Leon. I could smell your curse on him. That's how I knew he would feed you any information I wanted him to."

"At the O. Henry Hotel. You had Leon take us aside on purpose."

She shrugged. "I gave him a task to do, and I was not surprised that he shared the information with you. Hoped he would. Also, hoped he wouldn't. If he had kept his assignment quiet, then I would know his loyalty to me was greater than his fear of your curse. Either way, I benefited." Her mouth turned sharply down and all sense of joy on her face vanished. "I'm tired of you, Mr. Porter."

"Huh. My wife says the same thing."

"Your little jokes, your constant meddling, everything you have done since you moved to my state has caused me problems. And now, you're here — poking around in old history that has nothing to do with you."

"Since you and Grandma Mobley seemed determined to kill each other, it does have something to do with me. Because we both know that a witch war won't stay between your two little groups. A lot of innocent people will die."

"You see how little you know. A witch war won't hurt anybody but those directly involved. In fact, only the few idiots who get themselves caught up in the middle have anything to fear."

"She's referring to you," Drummond said. Then he twitched his head to the side. "She's up to something. I can feel a strange heat coming from her direction."

"Look," Max said, throwing on what he hoped to be a charming grin. "I know the Magi and I don't always —"

"No." The word held in the air like a roll of thunder. "Any chance of negotiations or reasoning is at an end. The witch situation in this town has been a powder keg getting fuller and fuller. You're nothing but a match running around wildly. I can't have you doing that anymore."

"I am sorry to have upset you."

"I'd say I'm more sad than upset. I thought after I cursed you that you would be more forthcoming in our relationship. And after you cursed Leon, I thought perhaps you might use that leverage to negotiate a better relationship with me. Instead, you've done nothing but work behind my back in an effort to undermine all that I stand for. How disappointing."

"You thought I should come to you with Crutchfield and this pest house? Why would I do that?"

"Because the Mobley coven is a bunch of witches. It's what the Magi fight against. It's what you were supposed to be doing."

Max turned his head to the side trying to pick up on whatever Drummond sensed. "Then I guess I'm the one that's sad. All these years and you don't seem to know the first thing about me."

Drummond said, "I'm telling you, she's up to something."

Mother Hope stood like a gunfighter ready to reach for her weapon. "I'm giving you only one opportunity — tell me where to find Crutchfield."

"I got here a few minutes before you," Max said. "He's not in the house. Maybe he moved on."

"Wrong." She flicked her wrist and whispered words Max could not hear. But he felt them. He felt the words heat the curse on his chest.

His lungs tightened and he gasped for air. He doubled over. His knees weakened, and as he collapsed to the floor, he saw Leon also dropping.

"You never took me seriously," Mother Hope said. "You always thought you would beat this curse. But of all people, you should have known better. You don't break a witch's curse easily."

"Don't worry, partner," Drummond said. "I'm going to take care of this." He hurtled towards Mother Hope.

She pulled a small pouch from her belt and threw it on the ground. "Goodbye, ghost."

When the bag hit the ground, a yellowish smoke puffed out of it. Drummond yelled as if he had stepped into the middle of a campfire. An instant later, he dissolved into the air.

Max tried to keep his eyes open. Tried to focus on Mother Hope, Leon, the room, anything. But his brain would not have it. His mind wandered. He thought of Sandra, PB, and J. He saw them crying, mourning their loss. And his mother — she would never be able to understand how he could be both alive and dead. But that was what awaited him. The curse would turn him into a ghost yet not a ghost. Caught between worlds. For as long as Mother Hope wanted.

All went dark.

Chapter 17

WHEN CONSCIOUSNESS RETURNED and with it the ability to see, Max kept his eyes closed. He had been here before. Cursed into a half-dead existence. Though he had always been cognizant of the terrible spell branded into him by Mother Hope, part of him never expected her to actually use it. Like all threats, its effectiveness died the moment of use.

He had always thought that if she enacted the curse, he would feel relief. The stress of having it hanging over his head would have ended. Yet now that it had happened, he felt numb. So why did he not open his eyes?

The answer galloped over him like a stampede of wild horses. He knew that his cursed condition did not end his involvement in the witch war. And even when the war reached its conclusion, he would get no rest. That was the true curse. Because he did not qualify as dead or as a ghost, there would be no moving on for him, no afterlife beyond his current existence. He would forever drift along as nothing more than a half-ghost.

But his brain reminded him of another truth. Regardless of his condition, Sandra would still be in danger. The Sandwich Boys would still be in danger. His mother, too. Max opened his eyes.

The first thing to strike him was the obvious — he floated near the ceiling. Gazing down on the attic floor, he saw his own body crumpled near the casting circle under the window. No sign of Mother Hope or Leon.

But the familiarity ended there. What had been an empty

attic now filled with the pale, ghostly afterimages of those that had come before. Twenty-four cots, twelve to each side, lined the attic walls. Men and women from different time periods lay in these cots, all in different stages of dying. Some simply slept. Others tossed and turned while coughing horrid phlegm-filled sounds. Still others rested flat on their backs, their faces and arms covered in red sores, their skin gleaming with sweat. Suffering flowed around the room like a foul breeze.

A tall, rather gaunt gentleman with a black derby walked toward the window. He stopped at Max's body and turned his head downward. Though he wore a tattered suit, he held his hat and his posture with dignity.

"Excuse me," Max said. "Up here. That's my body you're looking at, but I'm up here."

The man turned his entire torso around and arched back. Max waved but the man did not acknowledge him. Setting his derby back on his head, he ambled away — disappearing before he crossed the attic.

In his place, Max spied a group of large rats. Three gray vermin rushed along the side of the attic, keeping close to the walls. When they reached the far end, they regrouped, chattering to each other in a series of squeaks and clicks.

Max had a dark suspicion. *Please, no.*

One of the rats stood on its hind legs and sniffed the air. Max flapped his arms wildly but the rat took no notice. Instead, it scurried away from the wall and toward Max's body.

"You get away from me," Max said, but the other two rats joined their leader.

As these creatures cautiously sniffed around his body, Max shoved his arms out forward. Nothing happened. He kicked with his legs. Nothing happened.

He closed his eyes and tried to recall the last time he had

suffered from this curse. How had he moved? He knew it had taken practice, but he didn't have time for practice.

Relax. That had been one of the keys. Try not to overthink things and simply move.

He opened his eyes, and met the wonderful sensation of lowering to the floor. He drifted closer toward one of the rats — the leader. The little bastard had taken an interest in Max's fingers.

"If you so much as nibble on one of those."

Max had no idea how he succeeded — perhaps his anger, perhaps his fear — but when he slapped his hand at the rat, he made contact. The rat screeched and tore off across the attic. The other two rats jolted back, saw their leader take off, and raced after him. Their clicking claws scratched the floor as they skittered along.

For Max's part, an excruciating dagger of ice raced up from his hand, through his arm, and straight into his head. He curled into a ball and screamed. If he had the ability to form tears, his face would have been soaked. The pain receded after half a minute yet still echoed with the pulse of his blood. When he straightened his body and opened his eyes, he floated on the ceiling once more.

A young woman with dry chapped lips and death-darkened eyes stared at him from her cot. Max rolled his fingers in a wave, but she quickly looked away. He considered lowering to the floor again, approaching the girl, seeing if he could get her to communicate — even simply acknowledging his existence would be a plus.

But then Mother Hope's head appeared as she climbed the ladder into the attic.

Chuffing like an old steam engine, she made her way across the attic toward Max's body. Behind her, the new bodyguard, Annie, followed. Mother Hope walked a full circle around the body. She sniffed the air.

"I want him in the middle of this room," she said.

Annie cradled Max's limbs and lifted his dead weight with little more than a grunt. She carried him to the center of the attic, glanced back for a nod from Mother Hope, and plunked him down like a sack of grain. Max winced as his body hit the wood floorboards.

"Put Leon in the trunk," Mother Hope said. "I want you to drive him back to the O. Henry. Put him on ice. I may have a use for him later."

Annie made a slight bow and backed her way to the ladder.

Leon? Max spun in a full circle, taking in all of the attic. Clearly, before he had regained consciousness, Annie had moved Leon's body downstairs. She would take the body to a waiting car. But where was Leon himself? Shouldn't he be in the same state — a non-ghost floating around the attic?

Of course not. The curse tied him to his body. He would be outside.

Without giving it much thought, Max floated across the room. He slipped down through the floor and out to where the cars had been parked. When he realized what he had done, and with such ease, he grinned — *Like riding a bike.*

Standing in front of a new Lexus sedan, Leon watched his body being loaded into the trunk. "Look what you did to me."

"Mother Hope did this," Max said.

Leon swooped across the ground and shoved Max hard in the chest. "She didn't curse me. You're the fool who messed up my situation." He moved in fast, grabbed Max by the shirt and yanked him forward. "At least I'll have an eternity to beat you to a pulp over and over."

Annie started up the Lexus. Max said, "Sorry, pal. You won't get the chance. Better get in that car or you're in for a lot of pain."

As the car pulled away, Leon's head stretched towards it. The old man let loose a long, garbled yell as he tried to fight the energy tethering him to his body. But he had neither the strength nor the will to become a shredded ghost. With a sharp final cry, he let go of Max and zipped out into the night. Eventually, he would catch up with his body and his pain would stop. Max did not envy him the travel experience.

As the last red embers of Annie's taillights drifted into darkness, Max shivered. He was alone. He thought about all the ghosts he had dealt with over the years. Some of them tethered, some of them torn, some of them insane, some of them lost. Some could travel miles away from their bodies while others had a short leash that provided less movement than a prison cell. He never really believed he would end up among them. When he died, he had expected to move on. No logical reason to think that but there it was. Max Porter considered himself special.

He snorted a laugh. That was his mother in his head. He only considered his research skills special, and even those were a matter of practice and determination. He supposed debating his predicament had to be normal. He only hoped it didn't last too long. Then again, for a ghost or a spirit or a half-dead thing like him, time could twist in a nonlinear fashion. At least, that was how Sandra had explained it to him awhile back.

He would drive himself mad thinking about such things. He needed to stay focused on the present. He had just seen Leon get pulled back by his tether to his body. Max's eyes snapped open. He spun around to face the house.

He had a body. That body lay in the attic, and it was not alone — Mother Hope was there. Not a good thing. As he floated toward the house, however, he noticed glowing lights in the woods just beyond — pale blue, dim yellows, and stark white. Ghosts?

As he drifted around the corner of the house, he heard a gruff yet familiar voice. "Son of a —"

"Drummond?" Max squinted into the darkness for any sign of his old friend. As he came around to his right, a pale fist rushed towards his face. Despite his martial arts training, he failed to react. Drummond punched him hard in the jaw.

"What the heck are you doing?" Max said, spitting something sour — *did half-ghosts bleed?*

Drummond soared forward, his trench coat fluttering behind him. Max cringed, expecting another punch, but instead, the old ghost wrapped his arms around Max.

"I thought you were dead." Drummond floated back, sniffling and wiping at his eyes. "I mean real dead, not cursed dead. I mean —"

"I know what you mean. Where have you been?"

Readjusting his coat, he said, "After Mother Hope got her curse going, she whisked me about a mile out. Took me a bit to get oriented in the woods, and then I flew back here. What's been going on?"

"Not much. Everybody's gone psychotic on me and a witch is moving my body around like it's her personal doll. Oh, there's a witch war about to ignite, too."

"I've got to say — you're taking this really well."

"The curse? Heck, even if I survive this, once Sandra finds out, she's going to kill me."

Drummond managed to fake a grin as he gazed up at the house. "Yeah, but there's no guarantee you're ever getting out of this curse."

"I don't think it's completely sunk in yet. Don't worry. I'll have a complete mental breakdown soon enough. Until then, I figure it's best to keep pushing through. Maybe we can figure out what all is going on here."

"We know exactly what's going on — Mother Hope's gearing up for a battle with the Mobleys."

"It doesn't explain what any of this has to do with Crutchfield. Or why Mother Hope was so quick to enact her curse on me."

"Sorry to be the one to say this, but you may end up having a whole eternity to figure it out."

The lights in the forest flared up again. Max said, "What's going on out there?"

Drummond followed Max's gaze. "That explains where a lot of the ghosts are. Might be a cemetery out there. Or just a dumping ground."

"That's probably too far for my tether."

"No problem. I'll check it out for us."

Max put out his hand. "No. I've been stupid about all of this and look what happened. It's time to do this the right way. I should've told Sandra from the start. Will you do that for me? Go get Sandra's help?"

Drummond's face took on a serious calm. "You got it."

"One more thing. When I woke in the attic, I saw a whole bunch of ghosts, but you said you didn't see any there. How can that be?"

Drummond looked back towards the attic. "I don't know. I'll be sure to ask our expert when I get to her."

"Thank you." Max put out his hand.

Drummond cocked his head and raised one corner of his mouth. "It's been a long time since I've done something so human. Thanks."

As they stood shaking hands, Drummond dissipated. Max stared at the empty space where his partner had been, and he wondered how hard this curse would hurt Sandra. She would be mad but also terrified and worried. He hated that she would have to feel such pain. But, at least, he knew Drummond would find her. Soon, she would be coming to help.

"Together," he whispered.

From the other side of the house, the echo of a car door slamming reached Max. He had begun to hate that sound.

"Okay," he said to himself. "Who else could possibly know about this house?" Gliding across the clearing, he headed toward the front.

Chapter 18

MORE CARS ARRIVED as Max came around the corner of the house. Two Mobley sisters stood in front of an idling SUV while Jessica Mobley sidled up next to them. At the opposite end of the house, four Magi clustered together — two men and two women all in business attire. Both groups eyed each other like rival cliques at a high school dance — tense, ready to fight, but unwilling to strike the first blow. Except there were no chaperones to stop them, no police, no authority of any kind. Max guessed the only thing keeping them from attacking was fear of each other.

But then the front door of the house opened, and Max understood clearly. Lena Mobley exited the house and snapped her fingers at Jessica. The young Mobley sister hastened across the dirt road.

"Is everything set?" Jessica asked.

Lena spoke loud enough so that the Magi would hear her. "Grandma Mobley is upstairs with Mother Hope. There's no reason for any violence tonight."

Jessica crossed her arms and shifted her hip to the side. "I don't think the Magi feel the same way."

"I think they fear what Mother Hope might do if they start a rumble out here before the two ladies up there have had their say." Lena arched her head towards the Magi. "That right? Or is Mother Hope no longer in charge?"

One of the Magi women said, "We're not going anywhere. But if you try anything, we won't hesitate to take you down."

Lena put her hand on Jessica's back and guided her

toward the other Mobley sisters. As they walked off, Max's skin prickled — not from nerves but rather from magic. He sensed a change in the air. Something inside him, something based on his new existence, told him the feeling came from magic.

He faced the house as an orange bubble grew out of the walls like a nuclear weapon going off in slow motion. As the bubble continued to spread, the deep orange faded until it was translucent. And outside the bubble, he saw the ghosts that had been in the cots upstairs. They clung tight to the surface of this barrier. Max spotted Mr. Derby and the sick girl with the dead eyes.

They looked at each other confused and groaning in pain. As the edge of the bubble neared Max, he stepped back. Despite the pain these ghosts felt touching this magic, they continued to press against it.

Their tethers. The bubble pushed them away, straining their tethers.

Only if they're cursed. Without a curse, there was no tether. Max gazed up at Mr. Derby. They are cursed. That's why Drummond never saw them. Whatever the curse was, it made them invisible to him.

The realization captured Max's attention long enough that he forgot to move back. The dome of magic passed through him and continued growing. He stared at it, dumbfounded. Why had he been unaffected? He was cursed. He should have been shoved back, too.

Max froze.

The ghosts of the pest house were cursed, but they could not be tethered — their bodies were not in the house. Perhaps that was their curse — to be tethered without a body. He had no clue if such a thing existed, but he did not doubt that it could.

But the situation did not match his own — his body was

in the house. Whatever spell Mother Hope and Grandma Mobley had cast, it cleared out these cursed pest house residents, but they wanted Max around.

Feeling like a death row inmate walking toward his execution, Max slid into the house. He rose up through the ceiling and arrived in the attic. Mother Hope sat on her knees beneath the circular window. Grandma Mobley stood on the opposite side near the ladder leading to the first floor. And in the middle between the two witches — Max's body.

Both women had their eyes closed — most likely concentrating on the spell they had cast. Mother Hope broke her concentration first. She rocked back a little and placed her hands on her knees. "I didn't know if we could work together to make that spell."

Grandma Mobley leaned forward on a cane. "Maybe it was difficult for you, but I probably could have done it on my own."

"I see you've still got all your bite. You know, there are a lot of years between us. I have to admit that I wasn't sure this day would ever come. I often thought that maybe, one day, I would get through to you, but as the years have gone on, I figured the chances were dimming fast that I could wake you up to the wrongs you have done."

"The only wrongs I've ever done are because people like you try to control me. If you all had simply let me be, I would have never had cause to do anything to anyone. Besides, at least I'm honest about it. You hide behind your righteous Magi. You're just as much a witch as I am."

"I am nothing like you."

"Isn't that Max Porter's body on the floor? I didn't do that."

"That's a different matter altogether. And Max, if you're in here, you should know that you are going to be part of the solution to this feud. I figured that would make you happy. To know that your current state is not in vain."

Grandma Mobley chuckled. "You plan to use the energy of his body to give yourself an edge over me? How amateur."

"Your insults are not going to save you."

"Neither will that body save you. I can grab the energy off him far faster than you ever could. Doesn't matter how old I am. I'm better at this than you."

Max did not like anything he had heard. But worse than their taunting banter, they both suddenly grew quiet. Mother Hope pulled a piece of chalk from her pocket and drew a circle around herself. On the opposite end, Grandma Mobley produced her own chalk and drew a circle as well.

Both witches scribbled symbol after symbol along the edges of their circles. Grandma Mobley finished first and settled on her knees. She closed her eyes and a soft green glow formed around her circle.

Using her sleeve, Mother Hope rubbed away several of her symbols and wrote new ones. A blue hue rose from her circle. Grandma Mobley stopped her spell, turned to her side, and erased two of her symbols.

Back and forth the two witches played out this game. Each one trying to conjure a spell while the other reacted. Each reaction ending the initial spell and causing a new one to be formed. They never actually cast off the spells — they didn't need to. Their mastery of witchcraft told them how futile the results would be when countered by their opponent's spells.

Max watched this chess match of magic continue for over an hour. At times, the scratching of chalk symbols filled the room with deafening fervor. At times, they stared at each other with cold-blooded ferocity.

He wanted to break between them, disrupt their standoff, but he feared the result. He did not know which one of them would succeed, and he didn't know which one he wanted to succeed. Besides, he had no idea how he could disrupt things.

He knew he could physically touch them, but he did not relish the idea of enduring that pain. Plus, he had seen both witches dispatch Drummond with ease in the past. He did not want to think what they could do to him. And there was a greater concern, too — the witches outside.

As long as Mother Hope and Grandma Mobley continued their standoff, the Mobleys and the Magi outside would continue theirs. But the moment anybody outside sensed a conclusion inside, Max suspected battle would erupt in a volcano of spells.

Thinking about these forces, Max decided to check on everybody outside — make sure nobody wanted to hurry the process along. Sliding through the wall, he lowered to the ground.

The Mobley sisters had formed a large circle. They linked their hands around a small fire burning in a circle of stones. At the opposite end of the house, the Magi stood in military rows. Annie headed up the group, and from the front, she distributed charms and protection necklaces. Nobody spoke a word. Above, Max caught a glimpse of Mr. Derby, Sick Girl, and the rest of the pest house ghosts pressing against the dome.

In the midst of this standoff within a standoff, the crunching of wheels against rock echoed as a car drove up the dark path. It parked behind a row of cars and the engine stopped. Max drifted towards the new arrival, a sense of hope and relief filling him. He knew that car. The door opened and Sandra stepped out.

He could feel the smile growing on his face. He could

feel his heart lifting. But then the back door opened, and PB trundled out, his face gaping open in awe. From the other side, J came around the car, his face pulled down in concern.

Max looked at Sandra. "Aw, crap."

Chapter 19

BEFORE MAX COULD THINK, his mouth spouted off. "What are you doing bringing them here?"

Sandra put her hand on her hip and raised an eyebrow. "You are not really in a position to start fighting with me."

"The boys —"

"When Drummond came to the apartment and told me you needed help, I tried to leave but your mother stood in my way. Literally stood in the doorway. She's furious with you and me. Says we've been acting like she's at our beck-and-call. So, in her wonderful concept of wisdom, she woke PB and J and said that if I go out, then I have to take the boys with me. I think this is supposed to be a lesson — teach us that our lives have changed with these boys and we can't go running around partying all night."

"She said that?"

"Implied. I doubt she thinks I went off in the middle of the woods to talk to a ghost."

Hearing his wife call him a ghost reminded him of his predicament. All of his shock dropped away. "I'm so sorry this happened."

"With your mouth and Mother Hope's ego, I figured it was bound to happen eventually. What did you say to tick her off?"

"It's not about me. She's using the curse as a weapon against Grandma Mobley."

Sandra stepped back. "Grandma Mobley's here?"

Gesturing to the two preparing forces around the house, Max said, "I think everybody's here." He looked about the car. "Where's Drummond?"

With a slight shake of her head, Sandra said, "After he told me how to get here, he said he had an idea that might help. Then he disappeared."

PB puffed his chest in an obvious effort to fill himself with confidence. "Who you talking to?"

J yanked on his arm and made a shushing sound. "Can't you see something bad is going down?"

Max said, "Follow me. I'll take you to the safest place I can think of."

As he headed back toward the house, he heard Sandra say, "You boys follow me close. Don't talk to any of the people out here. Not a word. J's right. Something bad is happening here, and these people, because they don't recognize you, will assume you're fighting for the other side. They won't care how old you are, either. They'll kill you."

Max glanced back. He thought Sandra's words had been too harsh, but the way PB and J fell in line, keeping their eyes on Sandra like horses with blinders, suggested she knew more about handling them than he did.

As they walked toward the front door, Max heard rumbling questions cascade through the two groups. They all knew Sandra, and most likely, they knew of the Sandwich Boys, too. Max had to assume that both sides had performed thorough searches on him and his family over the years. But that didn't mean either group interpreted the information correctly. Sandra could be right — they might see the Sandwich Boys as a threat.

Once inside the house, Max led them to the kitchen. "Mother Hope and Grandma Mobley are both upstairs."

"Are you kidding? How does that make this a safe place for us?"

"Because nobody outside is going to dare mess with us

while we're in here. They won't even set foot in here until those witches finish this. Right now, up in that attic, they're in a standoff. I don't know how long it'll last, but being in here at least buys you guys time. I'll go check on them now. Make sure you and the boys stay here on the first floor. Do not go upstairs." As he floated through the ceiling, he heard Sandra instructing the boys.

At first glance, developments in the attic had eased. Neither witch hurried to dash off symbols on her circle. In fact, both sat quietly, eyes closed, concentrating deeply. To an untrained eye, the mood would have appeared sanguine.

But if anything, the tension between these women had worsened, and the spells they attempted to use had grown deadlier. Both witches had replaced their casting circles with triangles. Circles represented the unity of the universe and the cyclical patterns found within. Triangles, however, were sharp edged, violent shapes. Witches used that shape for casting dark and dangerous magic.

Most important to Max, his body remained untouched. Whatever Mother Hope planned to use him for, she either had backed off because of Grandma Mobley's threat, changed her approach, or simply hadn't gotten around to it yet. Max hoped for the former but suspected the latter.

When he returned to the kitchen, he found Sandra instructing PB and J how to aid her in setting up a spell. Not just any spell, of course. She wanted to re-create the spell she had used to save Max from this curse the first time. But back then, she had the help of a friend who also knew and understood magic. Also, they had his body. Those things were not true anymore.

She must've seen the doubt on his face. "I have to try," she said.

As they drew the casting circle, Max could not hide his confusion. The original spell she saved him with had been triangle magic.

Whether to placate the boys or answer Max's unspoken questions, Sandra said, "We're going to try a few simple things to get your feet wet. If those go okay, then I'm going to need your help with a big spell. Max is in trouble, and we're going to save him."

With chalk in his hand, PB scratched his face. "You don't really believe this, do you? I mean I know you guys have always had cases that deal with other people who believed in all this nonsense, but I never thought you bought into it."

"What I think doesn't matter. If it's like you say, then all that matters is other people believe it. That they see us doing this and they believe it."

As if he had suddenly comprehended algebra, he said, "Ah, I get it. We're putting on a show."

"Sort of. But it's very important that you commit to your part in it. You have to act like you believe. Act so hard that you kind of do believe. You understand?"

"You got it. We'll help Max no problem. But promise me that later you'll tell us what this had to do with saving him."

Sandra kneeled in the casting circle and wrote several symbols on the four compass points. She then asked PB and J to kneel at either side of her within the circle. Once they did, she clasped their hands in hers, closed her eyes, and muttered archaic words.

Max watched from the ceiling. He wondered if Drummond often felt as helpless as he did at that moment. People he cared about embarked upon a dangerous course of action, and he could do no more than watch.

Although Sandra kept her eyes shut, the Sandwich Boys regularly peeked. So when a white glow formed along the circle, PB's eyes snapped open wide. He leaped out of the circle and backed away as if facing an angry viper. "What was that?"

J pointed to PB's spot within the circle. "We're trying to help Max."

"I felt something strange. And I saw lights."

Sandra bowed her head. Max knew as well as she did that these boys were not up to the task. Already PB's mind began intricate mental gymnastics to rationalize away his brief touch with magic.

Sandra gestured toward the kitchen counter. "Both of you boys stand there. Don't move. I'm going to do this on my own, and I need you to stay there. Don't forget the dangerous people that are outside."

J did not let go of her hand. "I can help."

"That's sweet of you, but this'll be easier if I can concentrate on my own."

The boys pressed against the kitchen counter. "Not fair," J said. "We should be helping."

"Shut up, nerd," PB said, clenching his fists while his jaw quivered.

Sandra knelt once more in the circle and closed her eyes. It hurt to watch, but Max would not abandon her either. She had no way to succeed — the magic required to pull him back from this curse was too great for her alone. She knew it. Yet she tried anyway. And knowing his wife, this failure would hurt her even more than him. It broke his heart.

It took a few minutes and some strange expressions, but she leaned forward to her arms and gasped for air. "I–I'm sorry." When she lifted her head, Max saw the shimmering tears holding all of her terror. It wasn't just that she had failed at a magic spell — of course not. It was that she had failed to save her husband's life.

But then a voice cut through the room. "You're not as

good at magic as I was led to believe."

Mrs. Berkley entered the room. Gone were her stuffy, uptight clothes. She now wore a flowing outfit, brightly yellow and white with magic symbols on the trim. And her voice — her Southern accent had gone, replaced with a more worldly tone.

"Mrs. Berkley?" Max and Sandra said in unison.

"Oh, please. I am Madame Ti." She looked up at Max. "There never was a Mrs. Berkley and most certainly not a Mr. Berkley. If there had been, I would've seen him dead long before I worried about hiring the likes of you."

"You can see me?" Max asked.

"I should think that's obvious."

Max lowered to the ground, the puzzle slowly coming together. Sandra's brain moved a little faster. "You were the cloaked witch," she said.

"I was," Madame Ti said. "I thought that rather obvious, too, but you both are rather slow. It was a silly plan, I thought, but it worked."

Max said, "Why? What do you get out of doing all this?"

"I don't have to get anything. My employer asked me to do it, so I did."

Max did not like the way Madame Ti said the words *my employer*. It had a familiar, unsettling ring to it. It reminded him too much of —

Madame Ti stepped to the side and in walked a tall, stark lady. Her stiff movements matched her cold glare. She put out her skeletal hand and with a clipped way of speaking that Max knew all too well, she said, "It has been a while." She turned to the boys and made an awkward wave. "Hello there. I'm an old friend of Max and Sandra's. My name is Cecily. Cecily Hull."

Chapter 20

MAX OFTEN FELT GRATEFUL for having Sandra in his life, but he never realized how much before that moment. While he remained in a state of shock, Sandra stepped in front of the boys.

With a fierce scowl, she said, "You do not talk to those boys."

Cecily chuckled. Max had forgotten what an awful sound she made — like a wheezing old man barely able to make a squeak. "You ought to be careful how you speak to me," she said. "I am not ignorant enough to walk into situations that I do not have control over."

From his angle, Max noticed two burly gentlemen standing at the front doorway. The sight of her muscle cleared his head. She was no apparition. And she certainly thought herself vulnerable — otherwise she would have no need for hired thugs.

"How'd you get in here?" Sandra asked. "All those people outside would never let you in."

Madame Ti smirked. "They never saw us. It's an easy spell to cast when you have skill."

Ignoring the slight, Sandra kept her focus on Cecily. "What do you get from all of this? You've clearly gone to some trouble. You wanted us to look into Wilburn Walker. Why?"

"I should think that is more than obvious," Cecily said, running a bony finger along her chin. "Then again, you and your husband have proven more often than not that you rely on luck as much as intelligence. Perhaps you lack too much of the latter."

"We were smart enough to beat your whole family."

"Yet here I am. Oh, I readily admit that you and your husband had done a good job of ruining my family. We lost nearly everything. But, since I was always considered less than equal to the males in the Hull family structure, I had learned to protect myself long before I ever heard of you.

"I've always had special accounts containing enough money to live off of for a few years; I maintained some property — a woman needs a place to live; I always kept my own network of contacts for business affairs. And, of course, I learned to have my own relationships with those in the witch community. Not a lot to get going with, but a start nonetheless."

Max drifted back towards Sandra. "If she had all that, what took her so long?"

Madame Ti repeated Max's question for Cecily. She gave a firm nod in the direction Madame Ti pointed. "I'm sorry that I cannot speak with you directly. But I am glad you are here to witness this. As to your question — well, just because I had money and a witch did not mean I had the power to accomplish my goals. Over the ensuing years, the rebuilding began. When you unseated the Hulls, you created a vacuum. Witches were vying for power. After all, that's what is going on right here. The Magi and the Mobleys are fighting for control of magic in the area.

"If I was to take on all those organized groups in the beginning, they would have destroyed me. I learned a lot of great lessons from my family, and above them all, I learned to have the patience required to truly seize power.

"It also did not help that the economy grew too slowly. My investments provided enough to keep me comfortable, but the extra funds necessary to purchase loyalty were somewhat lacking. It was a rocky existence at best. Like living on a fault line in California. You just never knew when the ground might disappear underneath you."

"How poetic," Sandra said, taking the words straight out of Max's head.

"Things became easier when I met Madame Ti. She won't tell me where she comes from, but it's clearly not America. She and I learned that we had common enemies, and that made everything faster, smoother. While others flailed around, playing at magic and not truly understanding the power dynamics of the world we live in, Madame Ti and I recognized that the Magi and the Mobleys were the only two organizations to be concerned about."

Madame Ti rolled her shoulders back and lifted her chin. "Oh, yes, I've come a long way to see those two witches destroyed. We delved deep into the lives of Mother Hope and Grandma Mobley. We became like you, researchers at an extraordinary level."

Max held back a mocking laugh at their boasts. Seeing both women together, he understood why they had gravitated toward each other. Not only did both crave power through magic, but both held an overinflated view of self, and both were uptight beyond any normal level.

Cecily inclined her head toward Madame Ti. "We spent a long time doing that research. Months upon months of arduous work. But it was worthwhile."

"It's how Cecily devised her brilliant strategy."

Max said, "Wilburn Walker."

Cecily continued, "When the whole sordid affair came to our attention — the double murders, the rush to trial, and of course the unidentified man — we had a sense that this might be related to our witch friends upstairs."

Sandra said, "You found out how Mother Hope and Grandma Mobley were connected to William Crutchfield. You knew they hated that man for some reason. So, you had Madame Ti set Max up, had him find the name that would get us rolling on the whole story, right? You didn't even care what we found out — just that Mother Hope and Grandma Mobley learned what we were doing."

"Of course they would learn what you were doing. They both watch you very carefully. And, of course, the name William Crutchfield would draw their attention. I didn't know all the details at the time, but we found out enough. After all, he was a witch hunter."

"A witch hunter? Then why wasn't he going after them? Why go after Mary? Hold on. Mary Goins was a witch?"

"No. At least, she didn't think so. But others thought that Mary had the potential to be a powerful witch. Crutchfield decided to take it upon himself to destroy Mary before she had a chance to make that decision."

Max saw it all play out in his mind. Wilburn Walker and John Smith were merely in the wrong place at the wrong time. Crutchfield saw his chance to use them as a means of attacking Mary Goins. The shootout covered up his real purpose, and with his success, Crutchfield skipped town. Years later, somehow, he discovered the mistake he had made — that, in fact, Mary Goins was never a witch. Merely a sweet lady with a husband and children who did not deserve her fate. His guilt sent him to the police station in California. But after admitting his crime, he realized that if arrested, he would be sent back to North Carolina — home of two very powerful witches. The publicity of a murderer returning to face justice would certainly catch the eye of Mother Hope and Grandma Mobley. They would be waiting for him. He probably would never have made it to a jail cell. Instead, he came back on his own, taking a ship around South America. When he arrived, he had intended to hunt down Mother Hope and Grandma Mobley, to stop those witches from hurting others, but illness took hold of him.

Cecily knew the witch's hatred of Crutchfield would ignite their hatred of each other. After all, they both wanted to approach Mary Goins, and they both must have felt slighted at her loss. Not to mention the decades of resentment festering between their organizations. Once these witches destroyed each other, Cecily's group — no matter the size — would be able to clean up the remainder. Cecily Hull would resume power with Madame Ti at her side. Max doubted Cecily had expected her plan to work so well, but he also suspected she couldn't be happier with the results.

"Why send us after Walker?" Sandra asked. "You obviously knew the name Crutchfield."

With an impatient huff, Cecily said, "If I sent you straight for Crutchfield, those two gangs outside would not have converged here. Things would not have heated up enough. By making you take your time, it allowed enough paranoia to set in."

"Sure. Or you just like dicking people around."

Cecily gazed blankly in Max's direction — unable to see him — and said, "I did not know for sure if Mother Hope would turn on your curse, but I hoped she would. Partly, because you deserve all the suffering you get. But mostly because I need your help."

Max laughed. Longer than necessary — a sour note that rattled in his chest. And hearing Madame Ti explain to Cecily of his laughter, only made him laugh harder.

Cecily grinned. At least, Max assumed the creeping movement of her lips intended to be a grin. She said, "I understand your amusement. It is not unexpected. But you will help us. Somewhere on this property is William Crutchfield's ghost. What I need from you is quite simple. You are to find Crutchfield and get me his finger. Madame

Ti requires the appendage to perform a key spell."

"What makes you think Max would do any of that?" Sandra said.

"For starters, when he retrieves the finger, Madame Ti will be able to conduct a spell that will end the madness brought on by these witches. Bring back some order to this world."

Madame Ti bowed towards Cecily. "That is correct."

"And if your husband is still unwilling to help, then we have an alternative method of persuading him." She snapped her fingers and the two burly men by the front door thumped into the room. They moved fast for such sizable men, and in a swift motion, they shucked Sandra aside and grabbed PB and J. "Either get Crutchfield's finger or I'll see that these boys are cursed."

The boys let loose a wave of swearing. Sandra screamed out and raised her fingers. Max had no idea what kind of spell she could cast on the fly, if any at all, but she never got the chance. Madame Ti had prepared for this moment.

With a swipe of her hand, Madame Ti sent Sandra soaring against the back wall. When Sandra hit the wood, her body jittered as if receiving an electric shock. She slumped to the floor unconscious.

Max watched these things happen, shock keeping him from moving. He saw the men carrying off the boys. Thrown over the man's shoulder, PB pounded against his back but to no avail. J, however, did not resist. Instead, he stared directly at Max.

Chapter 21

LIKE A METAL PRESS SLOWLY PUSHING DOWN, Max felt his world crush around him. The boys taken, his wife at the mercy of a Hull, and he a cursed half-ghost. Only a short while earlier, it felt as if they were coming together, uniting their strengths, and though he had expected setbacks, deep within him existed a glimmer of hope. That had vanished like a ghost moving on forever.

The muscles in his chest locked in a constant state of constriction. He could only take short breaths. The skin on his face trembled as it tried to hold back his tears.

Then he remembered he had no tears, had no lungs, had no chest muscles. He had been removed from his body and thus, removed from the world around him. Everything had crumbled like an earthquake taking down a skyscraper — fast and merciless.

Madame Ti grabbed Sandra under the arms and dragged her limp form across the kitchen floor. Max swooped in front of her, waving a fist, and said, "Take your hands off my wife."

Rolling her eyes, Madame Ti said, "Protesting will not get you any closer to ending your torment. Do as Cecily Hull has asked and all will be fine." She continued dragging Sandra into the next room. She set Sandra across the wooden bench by the fireplace and rolled a jacket under her head.

"You see? I am gentle with her. Nobody needs to be harmed. Just go do as we asked."

"I'm not leaving until I get my wife and my boys back."

"I'm tired of you." Madame Ti closed her eyes and made a short motion with her hands. She muttered words as she lowered to the floor. Though she did not draw a casting circle, she indicated one in the air with her fingers. It only took a few seconds before she flapped both hands out once and yelled, "Be gone."

As if grabbed by a meat hook, Max hurled out of the room, through the walls, until he finished in the backyard. Sharp pain poked his chest where the hook had taken hold. Only Cecily Hull's laughter stayed with him — that horrid wheezing squeak.

He did not move.

Floating on his back, he made no effort to pick a direction. He peered up at the night sky and wondered where he had gone wrong, what misstep had he taken — because this was his fault. Sandra and the boys in trouble — that blame rested on his brow.

He wondered if Madame Ti's spell had done something more to him besides throw him out of the house. He should have soared back in and demanded his boys, put up a real fight, but another part of him whispered that it would have been a futile gesture. So, he floated.

"Come on, enough of this," Drummond's distinct voice called out.

Max lifted his head to find his partner in the air next to him. How long had he been drifting around, lost in this maudlin state?

As if reading his mind, Drummond said, "I just got here. What happened? Where's Sandra and the boys?"

Max felt that stiff grip in his chest once more. In a dazed tone, he said, "They — they took them."

"Damn. Knew I should've come up with her. This is all my fault."

"None of this would have happened if I had listened to

you and gone back to Sandra at the start."

Drummond turned away from Max, his head leaning back as he gazed up at the pest ghosts pressing against the dome. "That may be true, but after that point, I take the blame. Instead of joining Sandra to get back here, I went off to see Irene — not for anything torrid — went to ask her to drive up here and take the boys off your hands. Figured she could keep them safe at her house while we dealt with the witches. But I'm too late."

Max blew out a long breath. "It didn't matter how long you were. We had lost this thing before we even started. We were played."

Max explained as much as he could stomach recounting. He spoke in a solemn monotone, and when he finished, he sighed with an exhausted breath.

Drummond whirled on him and grabbed his shoulders. "What's the matter with you? Since when do you give up so easy? I understand you had a bit of a fright. I know you're worried about the boys and Sandra. That's why I need you to pull it together. Snap out of this and let's get to work."

"Work? The only real conduit we had to the corporeal world was Sandra. And it doesn't matter anyway. Everybody's been steps ahead of us throughout this whole thing. What's the point? They want to kill each other, I say let them. Cecily Hull wants to rule all of North Carolinian magic, have at it. Done. I failed to protect those boys and I failed to protect my wife. And to top it off, I have an eternity living here has a cursed entity."

Lowering his hat, Drummond took on a menacing stare. "We'll see about that. I'm going to give those folks a piece of my mind." Storming off to the house, Drummond adjusted his coat and flexed his fingers before making tight fists. He disappeared through the wall.

Seconds later, he came flying back as if shot out of a

cannon, smacked by the same magic that had tossed Max from the house. Rubbing his sternum, he said, "Well, I met Madame Ti and Cecily Hull. Those are two formidable women."

More than anything, Max wanted to find a quiet place set away from all of this nonsense. A couch or a bed that he could curl up on and close his eyes. Blot out the world around him. After all, what was the point in fighting when he knew the outcome? Drummond had said it right there — *formidable*. They couldn't beat a formidable opponent.

Giving his partner a weak pat on the back, Max said, "At least, you tried. Thank you for that."

Drummond nodded as he removed his hat and held it against his chest. "Looks like they got the best of us. Maybe if — but no, that wouldn't have worked. Anything we try is doomed to failure. I can see that now."

"I appreciate all you've done for us. It'll be sad to watch the Agency go, but I don't see it working well with both of us no longer on the mortal plane."

Drummond continued to nod for a moment. Then he stopped mid-nod. He shoved Max's hand aside. Slapping himself in the face, he said, "Don't listen to that voice in your head. Max, listen to me. It's a spell. Madame Ti did something to us."

"Of course it's a spell. She's a witch. One spell after another. Any hope we've ever had of fighting them meant using Sandra as our *de facto* witch. But that was never going to work. Look, you've been a great partner, and we had a good run."

"Don't do this. We're not saying goodbyes. We are not giving up."

Max let his focus shift away from the house. He saw the trees surrounding him like a slat wall that would ensure he never left the area. A prison. Reminded him of the clearing at the Devil's Tramping Ground where he had defeated Cecily Hull and Mother Hope.

"I'm not under any spell. You want to know the real problem? We destroyed the Hulls. We won. But here they are again. What's the point if we can't actually win? The Magi, the Mobleys, the Hulls — doesn't matter what they do to each other because in the end, one of them *will* win. One of them always does. And if not them, then some other witch or coven or group. But I'll tell you who never wins — us. Crutchfield was a witch hunter, look what happened to him. Your friend, Leed — an old ghost hunter — look what happened to him. Turned into a glowing glob and eventually killed. There is a long history of people fighting witches. But the witches keep coming back."

"Son of a —" Drummond chucked his hat into the distance, pulled his fingers into a fist, and coldcocked Max in the jaw. As his hat reappeared on his head, he said, "That witch's spell is making you say these things."

Rubbing his jaw, Max said, "Stop doing that."

With anger warming his pale face, Drummond loomed forward. "You need to get your head right. Those boys are counting on you. You understand? They don't have time for you to be caught up in this spell. Best thing a parent can do in life is be there, every day, steady as a rock. You want to be a parent for those boys? You've got to fight for it. Right now."

Max's heart pounded harder when he thought of the dangers the boys faced. Sandra, too. He worried about her terribly. But that voice from the back of his head — the one that did not quite sound like his own — though weaker than before, it still warned him that fighting Madame Ti and Cecily Hull was the definition of futility. He thought about laying his head down and letting it all slip away.

Drummond slapped the side of Max's head. "Do you

want to end up like all the ghosts we've met? The soldiers and the thieves, the mistresses and the Madames, the witches and the noble few — if you don't wake up and pay attention to what's going on, you'll end up exactly like them. And if you're going to become a ghost, you'd be better off following my footsteps. I mean, come on, haven't you ever wondered why I'm different?"

That perked Max up. "Why is that?"

"There it is. That spark of interest. The part of you that wants to solve a puzzle. That's why you are a great researcher. You want to dig down and find the truth."

"And what's the truth about you?"

With a shine in his eyes, Drummond said, "I refuse to give up. Even though every day of my life there's a pull on me — every single day."

"A pull?"

"It's like a crush. You know? When you're young and you have a crush on a girl and every part of your day there's this feeling inside of being drawn to her, of thinking about her, of wanting to be near her, of thinking about what life would be like with her."

"Like a stalker?"

"Like a crush. Don't be a jerk. Now, this feeling — I feel that every day but not for a girl. I feel it for the urge to move on. I'm not supposed to be here with you guys. You know that. Don't you remember? I could have moved on, but I chose to stay back." With a wistful note unusual for Drummond's voice, he added, "I did move on for a short period. Got a taste of it. I told you it was boring. And that was true. But also, it's beautiful. That's why I feel it every single day."

Max thought about all the years they had spent with Drummond. He tried to imagine moments in their past with this new layer of information. Times when

Drummond endured pain and suffering to protect his mortal friends — did he feel the pull then? When Max got the better of him with a sarcastic comment — did he wish to move on?

Drummond continued, "Don't you understand? I fight to stay here, all the time, for you, for Sandra, and heck, now even for those boys — and I don't even like kids. So don't give up. Your wife needs you, the boys need you, and I'm admitting to it right now — I need you."

Don't listen to him, that little voice said. *He's no better than Don Quixote. You want to go off to fight windmills? Even if you summon the strength for the fight, you'll lose anyway. Might as well just sit back and let the world do its thing. As you're going to die anyway, and the world will go on without you.*

Max locked eyes with Drummond. "I ... I want to fight, but I'm tethered to my body and all I know is that William Crutchfield isn't here."

Drummond winked. "But I'm not tethered."

It was a small statement. Nothing to it really. But having his last shred of a defeatist argument tossed away so simply, brought Max — the real Max — rushing back. He shot straight up, his eyes focused as he thought. "Madame Ti cast a spell on us. When she shot us out of the building. She made us depressed."

"That's right. You fight it."

"She made us convince ourselves that we had already lost."

"But we haven't. You only need to get your brain back here and we'll fight."

"I did. I'm here. We need to go find William Crutchfield and save our family."

Drummond smacked his hands together. "There's my partner."

Max put out his hand. "Thanks."

"Anytime. Now let's get to work."

"Just one thing. Can we never mention this spell and the things we said ever again?"

Drummond tipped his hat back. "I thought that went without saying."

Chapter 22

As the effects of Madame Ti's spell wore off, Max's brain fired into life. While this spell that created a defeatist attitude had weakened in a short period of time, Madame Ti had cast it rather quickly. They would have to be careful around her. And should Max survive the night, he would have to research this witch and where she came from.

The back of his head pulsated where the voice had been. Not exactly a headache but more like a remnant of a hangover. A glance at Drummond suggested he felt much the same.

Drummond put his hands in his coat pockets and hunched over as if he could contain the grim anger heating up. "How do you want to do this?"

"Just because I'm screwed by this curse doesn't mean Sandra and the Sandwich Boys have to be. Not that we can trust Cecily Hull, but I think she'll honor her word to this extent — she won't hurt the boys if we do what she asked. At least, this time. Once she's got what she wants, all bets are off."

"So, we find William Crutchfield?"

"Since I'm still tethered to my body, I need you to go off in the woods towards all those lights. See if you can find him there."

"You got it. And don't worry. There's a very good chance Crutchfield is out there. Those lights are definitely ghosts. I should know." Drummond gave Max a final squeeze on the shoulder before heading off into the dark woods.

Max paced a tight circle and worked over the details of the Walker case once more. If Cecily Hull told the truth, then Walker had been simply an unfortunate pawn. If he still had contact with the corporeal world, and if he had the time, Max could have gone to the library to research Mary Goins. But the more he thought about it, the more he decided that Mary and her husband would produce nothing useful. They were normal, everyday folks. Even if she had lived, from the little he learned of her story, Max did not think she would have joined up with either the Magi or the Mobley coven. Possibly wouldn't have believed the witches in the first place. And because she had no contact with Crutchfield beyond her murder — a notable point in her life but not one that created any knowledge of the killer — Max decided that any key to locating Crutchfield would not be found there.

No surprise. But he wanted to be systematic in his approach. That always provided the best results.

He glanced toward the second floor of the pest house. Beyond those walls, Mother Hope and Grandma Mobley continued their face-off. Every minute that did not result in an explosive burst of supernatural energy meant they were a minute closer to that exact thing happening. He had no idea how long those two old women could play out their game, but he could feel the clock ticking away. Feel it in his bones and hear it in the back of his head. At some point, one of them would make a mistake, fail to react to the possible spell of the other, and that would be it. Everything would go off.

Rubbing his temples, he leaned back. Mr. Derby and the rest of the pest house ghosts remained attached to the dome, longingly gazing at the house. They were like moths stuck to a screen door, straining to get closer to a light inside the house.

"One of you could be Crutchfield," Max whispered. Heck, Mr. Derby could be Crutchfield. Max had no clue what the man he sought actually looked like. A new voice spoke up in his head, but this one he knew well. His own little reminder when his brain thought he had found the right path to follow. It did not sound strong or confident at the moment which suggested that he needed more information. That would be easy enough to solve — the magic dome above him had a bunch of primary sources striving to get inside.

Pushing off the ground, an unnecessary motion for a ghost, Max lifted skyward. Off to his right, he spotted a bony gentleman with a mustache that would rival any modern-day hipster. The man's sunken eyes and shallow chest pointed to the ravages his body had suffered before dying.

"Excuse me," Max said as he neared the man. "I wonder if you could help me. I'm trying to find somebody who has been here for a long time. I guess you all have been here for a long time, but this one particular man joined in the early-1900s. His name is Crutchfield. You know him? Heck, are you Mr. Crutchfield?"

The man did not respond. Did not even look in Max's direction. He only had eyes for the pest house.

Further up the curve of the dome, Max came upon a portly woman with dark veins snaking along her face. Stains from popped blood vessels in her eyes darkened her expression.

"Ma'am? Could I have a few moments of your time? I'm looking for someone. It's important. It'll help save two young boys and a sweet woman."

The woman rolled to the side, turning her back on Max, and drifted away. Max wondered if she responded to him or if her turning away had been an accidental answer. He thought about earlier in the attic — felt fairly certain the ghosts did see him. But they clearly didn't want have anything to do with him.

He tried to recall things Drummond had said about the ghost community. A long time ago, there had been a ghost on the street corner near their original office. Drummond refused to talk to the guy because the ghost had been cursed. Or perhaps it was the other way around — that the ghost refused to talk to Drummond when Drummond was cursed. Max shook off his confusion. The point remained the same — regular ghosts and cursed ghosts didn't get along.

And I'm a cursed ghost. Well, a half-ghost anyway. Still, a curse was a curse, and regular ghosts did not want to get too close to those damaged by such things.

Max caught movement from below. At his vantage point, he could see the battlefield with the clarity of professional cameramen at an arena sporting event.

Even from high in the air, Max could see how the tensions played out. The Magi had taken a new position far closer to the Mobley coven. Four of the Magi had broken away and slinked around the back of the house. It looked to Max like preparations for a flanking maneuver — for when the time came.

The Mobley coven had also split its group but in a much different fashion. Nine of the women had stepped away from the large circle around the fire. They formed a wide half-circle facing their enemy. Each witch stood forward, hands spread wide at their sides. In the middle of the half-circle stood Lena Mobley. As intimidating as this could be, Max caught the real threat lingering behind by the fire. Three Mobley sisters continued to prepare spells at that location. But with only three, a circle around the fire was difficult to make. Rather, they joined hands to make a different shape — a more triangular shape.

Max saw clearly their intent. Each Mobley sister in the half-circle had prepared a spell earlier in the circle. Maybe even two spells. They now stood at the ready, armed with those spells locked in their heads, energy flowing, waiting to be released. Lena Mobley had spells too, but being more advanced, Max suspected she could juggle more in her head. And the three women preparing their own deadly spells by the fire — they were the equivalent of the Magi's flanking maneuver. A secondary attack from an alternate position.

If he did not find Crutchfield soon, take the man's finger, and deliver it to Cecily Hull, the chances for a peaceful resolution to any of this evaporated. Not that Max thought the chances were high to begin with, but anything would be better than letting these two groups loose upon each other.

For a flashing moment, Max wished he had been pushed back by the energy dome like the pest ghosts. At least then he could smack his hand against its hard surface. He could kick it. He could let out his stress no matter how futile the gesture.

He surveyed the pest ghosts, searching for anything that might clue him in on which one could possibly be Crutchfield. Clothing styles would have helped, if Max knew the difference between a 1904 men's suit and an 1897 men's suit. But they all looked rather old-fashioned and stuffy to him. Then his eyes fell upon Sick Girl looking directly at him.

"Hey you," he shouted.

With utter terror on her face, the girl spun away and flew off like a thief evading the police. Max tore after her. She moved fast as she skimmed the surface of the dome.

Though Max had become more adept at moving as a

ghost, he could not match the girl's agility. However, he could do something she could not — he could go through the dome. Dropping towards the pest house, he cut across in a strong straight line towards where he expected her to go. As long as she didn't notice his intentions and change direction, he would beat her.

Thankfully, her fear kept her on course. He saw her just above. She checked behind a few times but did not slow down. What had frightened her so much? Could it be as simple as the fact that he was cursed? He didn't know enough about ghost culture on a personal level to understand.

Over the final ten feet, Max spread his arms and lowered his shoulder. He burst through the dome right at the point when Sick Girl crossed his path. She hollered as he tackled her from beneath. His speed tossed her out into the air, and her hollers mutated into excruciating screams. She reached back toward the dome, toward the pest house, and her struggling made it difficult for Max to keep hold of her.

"Okay, okay, I'll take you back." With a gentle turn, Max slowly brought Sick Girl to the dome. When he placed her against the energy field, she pressed her face on it as if it were a life preserver and she a drowning victim.

But Max did not let go of her completely. No way would he afford her the opportunity to run away again. "I know you can see me. We both know you can feel me. And from the way you're looking at me, I know you can hear me. My wife and my boys are in danger, and you are all I have right now. So, I hate to do this, but I've got no choice. Either you tell me everything you can about William Crutchfield, and better still, point him out to me if he's here, or I'm going to grab you and throw you so far from this dome that your screams will never be heard again."

He wished he could say he had been bluffing, but part of

him was not so certain. Regardless, the girl certainly believed. She still felt enough social pressure to look around at who might be watching, but self-preservation overcame the possibility of ghosts ostracizing her.

She lifted one hand, her pasty skin hanging as if it wanted to separate from the bone. With haunting eyes and without warning, she thrust her hand against Max's chest.

The world dipped around him as a disturbing sensation rippled within. His eyes kept shifting directions. He couldn't focus. He tried to speak but his mouth had trouble forming the right shapes in order to create words. The smell of burnt toast permeated the air.

Am I having a stroke?

He had to remind himself that he no longer had a body. No body, no stroke.

The girl pressed against his chest harder. Like a bulb brightening before it burned out, the night sky turned white. Blinding. Max tried to shade his eyes, but the painful light surrounded his hands.

It all vanished.

He floated in the pest house attic. Mother Hope and Grandma Mobley were no longer there. Neither was his body. Instead, the pest house had been repopulated with cots and patients.

Sick Girl also hovered nearby. Along with several other ghosts, including Mr. Derby, they lingered in the air. The smell of rotting flesh, fouled bedsheets, and unwashed bodies created a vile stench.

Sick Girl focused on the scene below. Max followed her gaze to a young man wearing a stained white shirt and suspenders that held up plain brown pants. Max quickly surveyed the others, paying closer attention to details like their clothing, books they read, a newspaper. Most of the clothes were dark and plain — practical. He spotted three books — a bible, *The House of Mirth* by Edith Wharton, and *Sandy* by Alice Hegan Rice. He could not read the small print of the paper, but the style of the layout spoke volumes.

Max understood. Sick Girl was showing him a memory. But she was not walking the floor and not in a cot. This must have happened after she died. Floating on the ceiling, as she probably had done for decades, she watched along at what she wanted him to see.

Two figures climbed up the ladder and entered the attic. They wore dark hoods with robes that fell to the floor. On their faces, they each wore a crow's mask — a horrifying filter meant to protect the wearer from any infectious diseases, it looked like a long-beaked, big-eyed crow. Though he could not see their faces, Max had no doubt in his mind who stood beneath him — Grandma Mobley and Mother Hope.

The shorter of the two figures — Mother Hope — stepped forward and raised her hands. "We are looking for William Crutchfield."

The few patients with the energy to give Mother Hope their attention turned away. The others continued to stare off into space.

Grandma Mobley pushed Mother Hope to the side. "We know William Crutchfield came through here. If he's dead, show us to his grave. If he is alive, show us to him. You best do as we say, or we can make things very unpleasant for you."

From the back corner, a large man laughed — a harsh, wheezing sound. "Look around you lady. We're all in Hell waiting to die. You think you got something to threaten us with?"

He laughed again, this time his chortles turned to a mucous-filled cough. Mr. Mustache rested in the cot next to the large man. He only had the energy to smile. A few other patients chuckled, and even Mr. Derby made a noise that had a hint of amusement.

At first, Max thought they were all protecting Crutchfield for some reason. But the longer he watched them, the more time he spent observing their sickly faces, the more he understood that they didn't know or didn't care about Crutchfield. They certainly didn't care about the two women asking for Crutchfield. The concerns of each person in the pest house centered on survival, on finding comfort, on managing pain and suffering through the next minute. If they survived that, then the next hour. And for the lucky few, the next day.

But the witches would not see it the same way. They were focused on hunting down a witch hunter. Anybody standing in their way — or in this case, lying down in their way — had to be working against them. While the laughing man in the back had been right to suggest that everybody in the pest house had more problems than worrying about empty threats, he had been wrong to think those threats had no bite. Because even if the witches could not harm the dying, they could certainly harm the dead.

The two crow-faced figures huddled together by the attic ladder. A moment later, the one Max pegged as Grandma Mobley crouched to the floor and, with a piece of chalk she produced from within her robes, she drew a circle. Mother Hope walked in front of the circle as if an entourage's bodyguard. Nobody challenged her. Nobody had the energy or even the interest. At least half of the residence rolled onto their sides and attempted to go to sleep.

After a short time, once Grandma Mobley had the spell set, Mother Hope raised her voice. "Your final chance — tell us where to find William Crutchfield."

"Crutchfield, Crutchfield, Crutchfield," the large man in the back said. "Nobody cares about him. Nobody wants to hear from you. Go away."

Mother Hope reached high with both hands. "Then we curse you all. We curse you and this house. Not even death will bring you peace. You will suffer for eternity."

"I guess you're planning on talking to us until eternity, then, because it's sure suffering to listen to you." The big man coughed and laughed as Grandma Mobley set her hand on the circle and ignited the curse.

The two women climbed down the ladder, amused with their magic. Unable to curse William Crutchfield specifically, they opted to curse all the residents.

Max looked toward Sick Girl. "You're all tethered to the house because it's all you have left."

The world dipped again and the nausea-inducing shifts in his eyesight and equilibrium struck harder than before. He wondered if a ghost could vomit. He'd certainly seen Drummond make the motions but how did a stomach empty itself when it did not exist exactly? When the blinding light returned, he welcomed it because he knew it meant the disorientation would end sooner.

Sick Girl removed her hand from his chest. They hovered on the edge of the energy dome around the pest house. He had returned to the present.

Max turned his attention toward the woods. The ghosts out there, tethered to their actual bodies, must have been buried long before that moment. The others — their ghosts remained with the house while their bodies had been removed into the woods or some cemetery further away. And ghosts like Sick Girl and Mr. Derby — they had simply been caught up in the curse. Their bodies could be anywhere.

The worst part of the curse, however, was not the

tethering. The truly insidious part was that being unconnected to their bodies, they continued to suffer, never to know where they were physically located. Even if the curse were to be broken, moving on would be difficult until they discovered their resting places.

That was why Mother Hope and Grandma Mobley worked together to make the dome. They had to keep out the pest house ghosts; otherwise, they would have to fight off those angry spirits long before they could fight each other.

But there was one angry ghost that had never been cursed — at least, not in the same way. Max pressed through the barrier and zipped across the air, straight for the attic. He flew through the ceiling and found the two witch leaders still locked in their stand-off.

Things had changed.

The differences were not subtle. Grandma Mobley stood in her triangle with two black candles burning at her sides. Her left foot slid forward, bent at the knee with the heel off the floor. All of her weight pressed back on her right foot. It reminded Max of the martial arts stances he had learned in Tae Kwon Do. But this witch would not be performing any acrobatic maneuvers — at least, not the kind found in the martial arts.

Across the way, Mother Hope also stood. She had a single blue candle at the tip of the triangle, dark smoke snaking up through the air. With her weight evenly planted on her feet, she had her fists pressed together and her head lowered. She mumbled her spell like a mantra.

The air smelled different, too. The musty odor of an attic long forgotten had dissipated, leaving behind two competing odors — fresh cut wood from a newly constructed house and hints of the revolting stench Max recalled from Sick Girl's memory.

Grandma Mobley lowered her center of gravity as Mother Hope inched her foot back and leaned forward, ready to strike. Both women began audibly breathing — hard, slow inhalations and short, powerful exhalations. Like two angry beasts revving up to charge, their nostrils flared as they rolled their necks and shoulders.

Mother Hope lifted her head and opened her eyes — they glowed red. Grandma Mobley zeroed her attention on one strike point of her enemy. And her good eye glowed an emerald green.

As the glows pulsed with their heartbeats, Max knew this was it. After all their feints and calculations, their spells and rewrites, each witch had committed to a final move. They would only have one chance. They had picked an attack which the other clearly would recognize — it's doubtful either could fool the other — and both felt confident they would be able to defend, out maneuver, or in some way be victorious.

Max had to admit that part of him watched with the same fascination of watching an old Western shootout. If he really wanted to dig deep, he would have admitted that part of what kept him watching was the same draw in seeing MMA fighters brawl in the octagon — blood. Two great fighters, seasoned, knowledgeable, but in the end it came down to blood. Yet at his deepest core, at a place where the truth rested that he did not fear admitting, he wanted to know, had to know, the outcome. He had to see it for himself. Had to know beyond any doubt who would become his greatest threat.

A strange rumbling sound began, and it took Max a moment to realize that it came from Mother Hope. As the sound grew louder, Grandma Mobley began her own utterances. The hairs on Max's half-ghost arms stood up. He could feel the magic energy thrumming in the air, keeping time with the glowing eyes of the witches. That's when Grandma Mobley made a mistake.

She let her heel drop — a subtle movement but enough to warn Mother Hope that the attack had begun.

The low rumbling turned into a high-pitched warcry as Mother Hope burst into action. An instant later, Grandma Mobley launched forward. The two women charged with the energy, speed, and agility of Olympic athletes in their prime. All the magic necessary to give them that unnatural edge streaked off their bodies as they raced towards each other.

If Max had not been cursed, he would have died from forgetting to breathe.

Chapter 23

IN THE HALF-SECOND before the witches clashed, a thought hit Max with all the strength of a trampling rhino — he needed Mother Hope to win. She had created the curse that locked him in this half-ghost existence. While other witches might be able to patch him back together the way Sandra had once done, Mother Hope's skills were superior to almost all. Truly, only Grandma Mobley could be considered an equal. The only real chance he had to be completely free of the curse was through the witch that created it.

In the next half-of-a-half-second, Max saw Mother Hope's skin light up from within. Strange and archaic symbols flickered through her skin, seemed to burn their way out, in a sharp, orange light.

In the next flicker of time, Grandma Mobley shrieked across the attic, black smoke trailing in her wake. Her clouded eye cleared with emerald light and she salivated like a ravenous wolf.

In the final moment, Max saw his own body lift an inch off the ground. Wisps of gray mist pulled out of his pores as if his body smoldered but the smoke had nowhere to go. It tried to reach for Mother Hope, only to be lured back toward Grandma Mobley, only to be yanked back by Mother Hope. The end result — the smoke formed a winding gray path like a narrow mountain pass full of switchbacks.

As he watched this, he felt a tugging within his own chest. He did not want to know what would happen to him if either witch managed to gain control of that mist. He suspected he would welcome being a cursed half-ghost by comparison.

Both witches leapt into the air, crossing over his body, and when they reached each other, their magic exploded in a phosphorus-white light. A concussive force smacked Max against the ceiling — not through it but against it. The sheer power of their magic gave him solidity — at least, for a few seconds.

When the blinding light dimmed, he saw Mother Hope had dropped to her knees. She faced the attic ladder, wobbling like a spinning top about to fall. If she lost her balance, she would tumble forward through the hole in the floor. Probably break her neck in the fall.

On the other side of his body, facing the circular window, Grandma Mobley sat on her knees, gazing up at the moon. Like a hopeful princess, she let the moonlight bathe her. Her arms were open and resting at her sides. Her head bent to the right, letting her white hair drape her shoulder. She did not move.

Max watched one witch, then the other. Like following the ball at a tennis match, he bounced between the two, waiting to figure out who had won.

A creak of wood to his left. Mother Hope fell to the side. Her strained breaths spoke of a woman with only a few left.

"As it should be," Grandma Mobley said. She bowed her head, and Max heard an awful sound like the crunching of brown paper balled up and tossed away. Grandma Mobley's skin flaked off into little pieces. She let out one long sigh, and her entire body crumpled to the floor. Her skin, her bones, her hair — all turned to dust as if she had been cremated.

Max sped across the room, diving down to Mother

Hope's side. His own body had fallen back to the floor, as lifeless as the witches around him. No. Mother Hope still had breath in her.

She rolled on her back and craned her neck to look over at Grandma Mobley. A sadistic grin twisted her lips. "I win." Her wrinkled face softened as her eyes fell upon Max. "Oh. I see."

He did, too. If she could see him, then her life had neared its end.

"Don't do this," he said. "You've used me for what you needed. Please, have some decency."

Twirling a finger in the ends of her headscarf, she said, "I never could get the best of that witch. Even now, she gets the last hit."

"You can still break my curse. You could do something good to balance out all the wrong you've done."

Her hard stare returned. "Everything I did was to protect the world from people like the Mobleys. I should be made a saint."

"Then make your last act a saintly one. There's no reason my wife needs to be a widow. No reason those boys need to be fatherless right when they're getting parents. Come on."

He could hear the whine of desperation in his voice but didn't care. If she wanted him to sing like a showgirl craving any role on stage or cry like a baby needing its pacifier, he would do it. For all she had put him and his family through, no way would he let her die before freeing him. No matter what.

He grabbed her and gave her body a hard shake. "Have you lost all your humanity? Have you no soul?"

She hacked a loud, creaking noise from the depths of her lungs. Max let go, afraid his sudden outburst might hasten her demise. When the coughing fits subsided, her skin had reddened. He thought that to be a far better sign than if she had turned blue.

With one ring-laden hand, she gestured for Max to come closer. He inclined his head, pushing his ear towards her mouth. If she went Mike Tyson on him and took a bite, he swore he would find some way to curse her for eternity.

In a shallow voice, she said, "Cecily Hull is here, right?"

"Yes."

"I thought I smelled her disgusting aroma. No doubt she has asked you to find William Crutchfield."

Max nodded. "She wants me to get his finger."

"Makes sense. Well, you should do it."

"What?"

"Don't make a dying woman repeat herself. There's only one way left. You want to hurt that scab of a Hull, go find William Crutchfield's finger and use it. Give Cecily the finger." Mother Hope cackled at her poor joke, but it only lasted a breath. Her eyes rolled up and her head dropped to the floor.

Max stared at her. He waited. Any moment, she would raise her head with another body-wracking cough. She would finish her laughter and continue to mock Max with her long-winded words. She had to. And maybe, if Max found the right angle, he could convince her to break his curse.

But she did not move again. No matter how hard he stared at her, he could not will her back into existence. He had lost.

Except, if she died, he could talk with her ghost. He waited. The two bodies on the floor — Mother Hope's and his own — remained still and lifeless. The powdery remains of Grandma Mobley had no dream of returning whole. Other than himself, not a single ghost appeared. Which suggested they had gone somewhere else. He could not imagine that either witch had the clout to move on, but perhaps they had jumped to the Other right away. Or perhaps there were more planes of existence that he knew nothing about.

Because, without a doubt, neither witch was alive.

He could not have been sitting at her side for long, though it felt like hours. But soon the sounds that surrounded him returned to his attention. And those sounds were filled with screams and cries and violence. Max jolted straight up. Both witches had died — but the battle outside had only begun.

Chapter 24

MAX FLEW OUTSIDE and saw chaos. Like a machine gun, the Mobleys sent bolts of magic across the sky while the Magi used their protective charms to deflect the attacks. But no shield was ever perfect. Some of the bolts found their targets, cutting down several Magi with a horrid sizzling sound.

Max had never seen such violent magic. The Mobleys showed no mercy. Their blasts came down like grenades. Limbs were severed and heads removed.

But the Magi were not powerless. Annie thrust her arm into the air like a Civil War cavalry Lieutenant and bellowed, "Charge." The Magi stormed forward — a human wall of magic pendants, protective charms, and sharp blades.

Lena Mobley shouted commands and pointed at Annie. The Mobley sisters marched steadily forward. Balls of fire formed in Lena's hands and she catapulted them into the air. A young woman no more than ten feet from Annie went up in flames. The heartbreaking sound of her screams was matched only by the stomach-churning smell of her burning flesh.

The faces of the Mobley sisters opened in triumph — they thought they had won. But Max knew Annie's plan. The Magi's charge had more than one intention. They hoped to cause damage, but they also meant to distract from the flanking maneuver around the house.

Those four brave souls raced in from the side of the Mobley line. The forerunner, a gangly man, lunged his sword through the nearest Mobley sister. The Magi behind him ignited cursed objects or swung swords of their own.

As Mobleys fell, Annie's grin rose. Of course, the Mobleys were not without their own tricks. The three sisters forming a triangle at the fire sent streams of jagged green energy barking through the sky. When one stream came down like a bolt of lightning, it struck a well-dressed Magi hard at the top of the head and continued straight to the ground, short-circuiting his brain. He had a seizure, foamed at the mouth, and continued flopping on the ground while others fought on around him.

The whole thing struck Max as brutal and clumsy — amateurish — but it was war nonetheless. None of these witches had fought in such a vicious conflict before. Max guessed that if he did the research, he would find that the last witch war had been generations upon generations ago. These people knew nothing about what they had started.

A loud crack like the earth breaking open fractured through the air — but it came from above, not below. The energy dome created by Mother Hope and Grandma Mobley fell apart like a sheet of ice. The pest ghosts slowly descended through the air. With the casters of their curse dead, they knew that like Max, they had no clear or easy way to break free of their curse. Max spotted Mr. Derby and the sheer fury on his face twisted his entire body into a specter of rage.

The dread that permeated the area heightened as each ghost reached the battlefield. These ghosts did not care about the pain they would endure in touching the corporeal world. The time for vengeance had arrived — and if not against the witches that had cursed them, then against those who worked for the same witches. The ghosts swung punches, froze limbs, and attacked everybody on the battlefield.

Amidst this symphony of mayhem, Max hovered, watching it rage around him. Despite their various viewpoints, he wanted to help those who had fallen yet managed to survive. But there was no helping. If he touched them, he would only cause them and himself pain. Anyone that attempted to crawl on the ground or find safety beneath a car or near a tree, only found destruction at the hands of the pest ghosts.

Max spun back toward the house — *Sandra.*

As he blazed across the clearing, he spied the three witches by the fire. Their magic changed color turning burnt-amber. Before it launched, Max connected the change with the pest ghosts' arrival. The Mobleys and the Magi both would have been warned by their leaders that these ghosts existed. Mother Hope and Grandma Mobley probably left out a lot of details, but their armies expected an attack once one of the old witches died.

Burnt-amber spewed into the air with volcanic force. While witches and Magi fought on the field and others took cover behind trees, rocks, and cars, this brightness called all eyes upon it with the awe of a fireworks finale. As the lava-like pillars of energy split and broke away, pest ghosts began to wail.

The portly ghost that turned her back on Max became a standing post of fire. All those who could not see ghosts could easily see the outline of a person aflame thrashing in anguish. More of the spellfire dropped on the ground, and the pest ghosts scattered.

Max dodged and weaved as he hustled for the house, but something planted a burning kick on his back and sent him into the ground. He cried out, the fire shooting up his spine into his head. His momentum saved him — that, and the fact that he was half-ghost.

Because he did not stop moving when he hit the ground.

He broke right through, soaring deep into the clay with the ants and worms. While he moved with ease, the fire upon his back still followed the properties of the corporeal world. Being underground snuffed out the flames.

Max thought about traveling under the house, avoiding the battlefield altogether, but he had no idea what direction he faced or how to judge the distance. His mind did not like it either. He knew he did not need to breathe, yet his chest tightened and he could feel claustrophobic panic rising.

With an unconscious shove, he blasted upward until he reached the surface. The pest ghosts that had survived the initial assault had taken cover. The battle raged on but a few had become less brazen and more sensible in their bloodlust.

Several feet away, he saw Madame Ti and Cecily staring out the corners of the first floor windows. Not far to Sandra now.

"Max, over here," Drummond called from the corner of the house.

Gesturing to the house, Max said, "Sandra."

Drummond understood. He shot off faster than Max had ever moved as a ghost and cut through the walls. When Max finally caught up, Drummond hovered in front of Sandra like a pale bodyguard.

"I take it the fight upstairs is over," Drummond said.

Max paused to catch his breath, but then noticed he felt fine. Of course — he had no breath to lose. "They're both dead."

"That explains everything outside."

Madame Ti stepped toward Max. "Where is the finger?"

Max raised his middle one. "Here's a finger."

"Insult me again and see what happens."

Exerting great willpower, Max bit back his next five

retorts. At length, he said, "You want Crutchfield's finger, then you make sure nobody comes through that door. We'll get it for you." Turning back to Drummond, he added, "Please tell me you know where Crutchfield is."

"Well that depends on whether you want good news or bad news."

"Damn. We're screwed."

"Hold on, hold on. It's not that bad. I didn't find him because he isn't there."

"But he has to be around here somewhere."

"Maybe he was one of the lucky few who actually got better and was released from the pest house."

"No." Max told Drummond about his run-in with Sick Girl and all she had revealed.

Drummond tapped his chin. "That's why I didn't see those ghosts. Their curse kept them from being spotted. Must be an extra little bit of pain the witches wanted to give them. But you're not a full-on ghost. Guess the blinding part didn't apply to you."

"Yay for being a half-ghost. Look, all of this adds up to the fact that Crutchfield has to be among those ghosts. I've already asked around several of them, but I can't get them to talk."

Drummond lowered the brim of his hat and adjusted his tie. "Allow me. I'll get them to talk." Snapping his fingers at Max, he added, "You stay here and protect Sandra. Those pest house ghosts are very angry, and they're not going to care that Sandra is with you."

Drummond raced out of the building, and Max paused to look over his wife. She wrinkled her nose — possibly from an itch, possibly from a dream. She looked so lovely and peaceful, unaware of the war erupting around her. *Hang in there,* he thought. *We're going to get through this.*

He hoped his thoughts would be the truth.

Chapter 25

WITH EVERY TERRIFIED SCREAM, every metallic clang, every unnatural sizzle, Max flinched — his eyes locked forward, his ghostly body taut, ready to defend his unconscious wife. He needed her more than ever. Her abrasive sass, her alluring smile, her deep and gentle heart — having her at his side strengthened him, gave him confidence.

"Madame Ti, I know you can hear me. You need to wake Sandra up."

"Shut up, ghost." Madame Ti peeked out the window and dropped quick. A flash of green light filled the pane.

"End your spell on her. Wake her up. She can help us. Or are you so pigheaded that you'd let your employer die at the hands of all those crazy people out there?"

Using her own chalk, Madame Ti drew a hasty circle around herself and scribbled several symbols along the outer-edge. "You want your wife back? You want your boys? You know what you have to do."

"We're getting you that finger, but my wife will save all of our lives."

"I hardly need her." Resting a hand on the circle, Madame Ti closed her eyes and mouthed the words to her spell.

Something pounded against the wall. It could have been a spell attacking the house. It could have been a body thrown against the outside wall. Clearly, it could not have been anything good.

Max hovered over Sandra. He raised his hand, concentrated on making it solid, and quietly apologized to his wife. In a fast motion, he slapped her across the face. A jagged, burning pain raced up his palm, through his arm, and straight to the phantom bones within his phantom body. He moaned as he flexed his fingers. But when he looked back, Sandra remained asleep.

From behind, Madame Ti let loose a ferocious growl. Max turned in time to see her haul off a cannonball-sized chunk of glowing blue energy. It went right through the fireplace like a ghost. Though he could not see the result, he certainly heard it — tortured howls erupted only seconds later.

Cecily Hull surprised Max. He thought she would spend the entire battle crouched in the corner. But as the fighting wore on, she adapted. Though she looked tense, her hands beat out her impatience against the wall.

"Enough of this," she said. From her purse, she pulled out a .38 revolver. Breaking the bottom corner of the window pane with the butt of the weapon, she shrieked, "You're all going to die." Sticking the muzzle out, she opened fire.

Before the third shot went off, Madame Ti tackled Cecily, bringing her down away from the window. The glass shattered inward and a bolt of green energy smashed into the far wall.

Madame Ti said, "You can't bring a gun to a magic fight."

"That's a ridiculous thing to —"

The front door burst open and two ghosts slipped through before Madame Ti could close it — not that they needed an open door. The first ghost, a short balding fellow, rushed at Madame Ti. As he crossed her casting circle, she raised her hands and shouted words that echoed throughout the room. The ghost froze, straining against some unseen power yet pushing back hard enough to cause

Madame Ti an equal strain.

The second ghost launched after Max. The man zipped across the room, all muscle, all rancor. He must have been a professional wrestler in life or a full-time bouncer. Either way, to Max it meant trouble. And pain.

The first two punches landed hard on Max's sides. Had he been alive, those fists would have broken his ribs. Instead, the vicious strikes jarred his body. A third punch connected with Max's sternum, throwing him through the archway into the kitchen. As this bruiser ghost followed up for another attack, Max remembered something vital — in his life, he had been training in martial arts. Nearly reached his black belt.

Centering himself, he settled into a fighting stance. The first problem became immediately apparent — he had no weight. Most martial arts moves worked because of how the fighter balanced his weight, how he shifted the weight through a punch or kick, or how he used his opponent's weight against him. Except neither Max nor his opponent had any weight.

But I still know the moves.

Bruiser hauled off with a haymaker, and Max had no trouble ducking the punch. Coming back up, he planted his knee in Bruiser's gut. Bruiser grunted and attempted to swing back, but Max simply grabbed the arm and continued the motion, tossing Bruiser through the wall.

The move would have been impossible to manage if Bruiser weighed what his size indicated. Max didn't think the effort had caused much damage, but at least, it gave him time to reset for another attack. But it did not come. Max stood at the wall waiting for the return of his opponent, yet nothing happened. Blind rage had worked in his favor. Bruiser probably did not care who he fought, only that he inflicted pain. Outside, he must have found another target to satisfy his needs.

Sandra.

Max rushed back to the front room to find his wife safe on the bench. Madame Ti kneeled in her casting circle and prepared another spell. Whatever happened to the short, bald ghost, Max never would find out.

With all the calm of a Sunday stroll, Jessica Mobley sauntered into the house. Her face, however, showed none of the relaxation in her body. The cords on her neck stood out and her jaw pulsed as she ground her teeth. To Madame Ti, she said, "You're a traitor to your own kind."

Madame Ti stayed focused on her next spell. To his surprise, Max watched Cecily leap forward. In her hand, she carried a switchblade — the woman had certainly come prepared. She snicked out the blade as she swung her arm toward the Mobley witch.

Jessica moved as if she existed on a different plane of time. Graceful and fluid, she stepped aside and smoothly disarmed Cecily. She used no martial arts that Max had ever seen. She barely touched Cecily. Whatever magic controlled Jessica, Max doubted that Madame Ti would be up to the challenge.

Jessica raised her hand. In it, she held Cecily's switchblade. Before his mind could form a cohesive thought, Max shot forward. On an instinctual level, he understood that to lose Cecily Hull meant losing the help of Madame Ti — not an acceptable outcome. Without Hull and Ti, Max would be reduced to begging for help from Lena Mobley, and no Mobley would help Max find a way through his curse. Not anymore.

Using the same casual grace she had displayed thus far, Jessica brought her arm down, striking at Cecily's neck. Before she hit, Madame Ti swung out her hand as if lobbing a softball — but this contained magic. It struck

Jessica's arm and sent the blade spinning off to stick in the wall.

Jessica strolled up to Madame Ti. "It's a shame. With the talent you possess, you could have been a great asset to the coven. Instead, you're just a traitorous bit—"

Max had never attempted to freeze a person's brain before. He had seen Drummond pull off the technique numerous times, and he knew enough to expect terrible pain in retaliation. As he penetrated Jessica's skull with his hand, it occurred to him that he had no idea if Drummond used a special twist of the wrist, a careful flick of the finger, or a unique opening of the hand. He knew enough not to make his hand solid. Logic told him that would scramble the woman's brain, not freeze it. But like all else he had discovered so far as a half-ghost, he merely had to concentrate on the results he desired and his "body" knew what to do.

Jessica's limbs stiffened. Her head snapped upward. And she toppled to the floor, unconscious.

Max toppled next to her. He clamped his hand against his stomach and curled into a ball. Every part of him burned and chilled simultaneously. It seemed that even his hair hurt. His vision blurred for several breaths, and when he could see again, he spotted Sandra rolling to her side — comfortable and serene.

To Madame Ti, he said, "Have you had enough? Wake her already. Get her help."

Madame Ti hesitated. Max would take that as a positive step in the right direction. But then the witch dropped her eyes on Cecily. She rushed over to her employer and helped the woman up. No help would be coming for Sandra.

Bright red smoke drifted by the front door. Some of it got caught in the air currents and slipped inside the house. Max stepped toward the entrance. He could not tell if the

Magi had brought smoke grenades or if the colored fog came as a result of a coven spell.

Though it dampened much of the sound, it did not completely mute the battle. The crying, the pain and groans, the grunts of fighting — it all mutated in the red fog. It became an otherworldly experience of disembodied noises. Voices of battle invisible to the eye.

It held a strange beauty like an abstract painting with enough grounding that it created an emotional response. It felt good not to stress or fear. Despite knowing where those sounds must lead to, Max reveled in the momentary respite.

Until one of those garbled yells became clearer. And closer.

Bursting through the smoke — Sick Girl. With her arms outstretched, she lunged at Max like an enraged panther. He tried to jump back. As she slammed into the room, she shoved Max aside and attacked the walls.

Ignoring the obvious pain her actions caused, she hacked at the wood until she made a sizeable hole. Reaching in, she grabbed planks of the wall and yanked it apart. Splinters flew into the air as she tossed aside chunk after chunk.

At first, Max thought she had finally lost her mind. But it became evident that her rage was not misdirected. She attacked the house itself.

For Cecily Hull, the wall must have appeared to rip itself to pieces. She knew enough to recognize the work of a ghost, but she had not the experience yet to find it commonplace. Or perhaps it was her fear left over from nearly dying at the hands of Jessica Mobley. Either way, Cecily rushed into the kitchen to get away from the self-destructive wall.

Madame Ti stepped into her casting circle and raised her

hands in Sick Girl's direction. Closing her eyes, the witch began another spell. Wrong move. Sick Girl never wanted to see another witch again — ever.

With a piece of the wall in her hand, Sick Girl pulled back and swung it like a baseball bat. She cracked Madame Ti on the side of the head. Madame Ti plunged to the floor, blood dribbling from cuts on her face. She looked dazed but not dead.

Sandra groaned as if she had been hit, too. Sick Girl turned in a circle, her eyes seeking out a new victim. Max knew she had only one other human choice — Sandra.

He jumped in front of Sick Girl — well, swished across the air — and grabbed her by the shoulders. "It's me. You remember me?"

In her fugue state, she did not appear to recognize even her surroundings.

He gave her a shake. "Pay attention. Look at me. You showed me your memories."

She tried to gaze over his shoulder, to target Sandra.

Max spun her around so that her back faced his wife. He then lifted Sick Girl up to the ceiling — anything to change her perspective. "I understand how you feel. I know what it's like to be cursed. And I know how you felt when you were alive."

Her brow knit as if she struggled to decipher his words.

"It's true. When I was little, I got terribly sick. Not exactly like you. Nothing incurable. But at the time, I didn't know that. I ran a fever — a high fever. So high, in fact that the doctors told my mother to give me an ice bath."

Sick Girl's eyes widened.

"Oh, you've had one, too."

She nodded.

"Then you know how awful an experience that is. Almost as bad as touching the real world as a ghost. I nearly died then. Even afterward, I spent over a week in bed with barely the energy to move. It was a horrible experience, and I didn't even have to deal with a witch threatening to curse me. But later in my life, I met Mother Hope and she did curse me. That's why I'm here now like this."

He could see the girl he knew returning. Her face slackened. Her eyes softened.

"I don't know how this is all going to end, but I can make you this promise. If I can get ahold of William Crutchfield, there is a slim chance I can help you. And I promise I'll do everything I can to make that help worthwhile. But I have to find Crutchfield or nothing will happen."

She swallowed hard, and it occurred to Max that perhaps she was afraid of Crutchfield.

"I know he's one of you from that attic. He has to be. Please, all you have to do is point him out to me."

Two ghosts crashed through the ceiling, nearly clobbering Max as they spun to the floor. As the ghosts rolled over, Drummond locked his arms around Mr. Mustache. Sick Girl tapped Max on the shoulder and pointed at Mr. Mustache.

Drummond said, "I think I've got Crutchfield."

Chapter 26

THE STRUGGLING GHOSTS wrestled a foot above the floor. Crutchfield, a.k.a. Mr. Mustache, snarled as he threw an elbow back into Drummond's side.

"I can't hold him forever," Drummond said. "You want that finger, take it now."

"How?" Max said. "Is there some kind of ghost-knife that'll cut a ghost-finger?"

"You don't know how? I got him here. I did my part. Figure out the rest."

Covering her mouth in shock, Sick Girl hastened out of the house through the far wall. Madame Ti and Cecily had their attention glued to the fighting outside. Cecily could not see the struggling ghosts, of course, and if Madame Ti heard any of it, she gave no indication. Max and Drummond were alone.

Crutchfield slipped from Drummond's grip. As he made to escape, Drummond swept ahead and clotheslined the old ghost. Crutchfield went down and Drummond leapt on top of him.

Max's thoughts raced through one possibility after another, desperate to find a solution. If he wanted to cut off a ghost's finger, he had to have a way to make the ghost solid. But how could they force Crutchfield into being solid? There probably existed a spell for it, but unless they could subdue Crutchfield, Max didn't think Drummond would be able to hold on long enough for Madame Ti to perform such a spell — if she would willingly do so in the first place. Just because the witch and her employer wanted the finger, didn't mean the witch would make it easy. They rarely did.

A distasteful idea popped in Max's head, and as much as it turned his stomach, he knew it would be their best chance at the moment. The only thing that could touch a ghost with ease was another ghost. Max could grab Crutchfield's finger and attempt to snap it off, but while he had the strength to break the bone, he doubted he could tear it free during a struggle.

But he could bite the thing off.

Refusing to give himself time to back out, Max dropped down to Drummond's side. He locked Crutchfield's wrist with his arm and grabbed for the man's index finger.

"Foul servants of evil," Crutchfield said as he balled his fingers into tight fists.

The three men hovered in the middle of the room, revolving like some bizarre mobile. Max tried to dig into Crutchfield's fist, tried to force one of the fingers free, but each movement spun them at one angle then another.

"Hold him still," Max said.

"Gee, really?" Drummond said. "I figured you were having a fun time down there and wanted me to flip around some more."

Through gritted teeth, Crutchfield said, "Fools. You'll burn in the fires of Hell for this."

Out of frustration and necessity, Max flattened his hand and chopped fast at Crutchfield's ribs. The sudden attack forced Crutchfield's muscles to spasm. Max got hold of the man's ring finger and wrenched it back.

Bent over the finger, mouth open, Max winced at the idea of finding out what a ghost-finger tasted like. At least, his mouth would not be full of blood. Lowering his head, wanting to retch yet knowing he was incapable, Max bared his teeth.

He heard the attack just before it struck — a high-pitched whine like a bottle rocket. A blast of fire-red magic shot into the room like a javelin. It hit the floor and its energy walloped into Max, gyrating him head over heels until he ended up with his legs hanging outside the house while his upper-half poked through a kitchen cabinet. His head felt thick, and he strained to understand how to move. But a few seconds later — a minute at the most — his brain cleared, and he brought his aching-self back fully into the house.

He found Drummond on his side, one hand stretched out, gripping Crutchfield's shirt. Crutchfield jerked his body hard and broke free. He flew out the front door, back into the smoke-filled battlefield.

Max helped Drummond up. "He's getting away."

"I'm fine," Drummond said, holding his right arm against his side. "Let's go, let's go."

Drummond shot outside. Max started to follow but made a swift detour to Madame Ti. Swiping his hand across her shoulders, giving her enough chill to recognize his need for her attention, he said, "You watch over my wife. Anything happens to her, and I'll find every way I can to destroy you."

He did not wait for a response. Crutchfield had to be caught, and Drummond was in no shape to do it on his own. Max bolted into the fog.

Much of the smoke had broken up and drifted off into the woods. Patches floated by like new mutations of ghosts. Moonlight, headlights, and firelight cut through the remaining smoke to create strange shadows and disturbing shapes on the ground and near the trees. Some of those shapes turned out to be rocks. But others — what remained of the participants of war.

Seasoned soldiers would have ended this battle already.

But the Magi and the Mobleys had poor aim and little training. As battle plans broke down and communication lines weakened, the survivors found themselves lost in smoke and striving for any sense of what to do. Soaring across the carnage, it seemed to Max that one of the worst horrors of any battle was the uncertainty.

He searched the area for Drummond or Crutchfield. He caught shadows elongated by moonlight running off, but only people needed to run. And a ghost did not cast a shadow.

Drifting toward the cars, Max came upon the heavyset Magi who had guarded Mother Hope's door at the O. Henry Hotel. He sat in a pool of blood, his vacant eyes and drawn lips granted him a childlike appearance. But Max did not see any injuries to the man — the blood did not belong to him.

These people had never been prepared for war. Most had joined the Magi because of some personal experience with the supernatural. They joined to aid Mother Hope and those with the skill to fight such dangerous paranormal entities. But many of them operated in very mundane ways — guarding doors, operating the hotel, running surveillance on individuals. Probably few of them ever encountered actual action. Until now.

It was the key difference that gave the Mobleys an edge. Every single Mobley was a witch. Every one of them had direct contact with magic. They had understood exactly what could be expected from battle. With only thirteen sisters, they were outnumbered, but held their ground through skill and knowledge.

Yet several feet away, Max came upon the corpse of a Mobley sister. Her arm had been shorn from the elbow down and a blade had cut open her neck. The shock frozen on her face rang of her disbelief that death could have come for her.

And in all of this, Max could not find a hint of Drummond or Crutchfield. By now, they had probably run deep into the woods and Max would have to rely on Drummond to save the day. He wanted to go after them, but the tether to his body would stop him.

Hold on — Crutchfield was every bit as cursed as Max. Like Sick Girl and Mr. Derby, Crutchfield's body had disappeared but his tether remained.

Rushing back to the house, Max tried to picture the cots lined in the attic. As he broke through the front wall and lifted into the air, he pressed his memory to pick out where Mr. Mustache had been stationed. He blasted into the attic and reached the ceiling. Gazing down as he had when experiencing Sick Girl's memories, he strained to recall each person in each cot.

His skin crawled at the sight of his own body as well as Mother Hope's corpse and Grandma Mobley's ashes. He watched his stomach and chest. Once he saw the rise of a breath, he blotted the image of the bodies from his mind.

Instead, he imagined the cots spread out in their careful rows. He saw Sick Girl on her back with her sunken eyes. He saw Mr. Derby aimlessly pacing the aisle. And the big man in the back corner who mocked Mother Hope, his laughter breaking down into body-shaking coughs.

There. In the cot next to the big man. Mr. Mustache rested on his side, shivering despite the heavy blankets atop his gaunt form.

Whisking across the room, Max zeroed in on the spot. He looked closely at the floor where the cot had once been. Nothing but dust. He gazed up at the ceiling rafters. Perhaps Crutchfield had carved something important, but the wood had been untouched.

Max rushed up to the ceiling, bringing his face close to

the wood. He inspected the nails that stuck through, the slivers of rough wood that had splintered off, the soft dust mounding on the top side of the beams. Something had to be here that connected to Crutchfield. Why else would Madame Ti and Cecily Hull be here? They could have waited anywhere for Crutchfield's finger to be delivered, but they risked their lives to be in the middle of a witch war. Perhaps it made sense at first — they wanted to be ready to fight whichever leader survived, but with both Mother Hope and Grandma Mobley dead, Cecily and Madame Ti could have left before the clash erupted. They could have counted on Max to get the finger and taken hold of it at their leisure. They could've waited a day or two for the violence to recede.

Instead, they crouched in the corner downstairs, pressuring Max through his family to get the finger and get it to them in the house, right away.

It had to be more than the house. Yes, the curse hit all those connected to the house, it tethered the ghosts to the house, but for Crutchfield it had to be more. If not, then why not use any ghost's finger who was cursed to the house? Of course, Cecily might simply revel in the poetic justice of attacking Crutchfield, but Max's intuition suggested otherwise. Something in the house —

In the house?

Max dropped to the floor, paused, then plunged his head into the wood. In the gap between floor and ceiling, he saw a tin box no bigger than a sardine can. Mounds of dust sat upon it as if it had not been touched for over a hundred years.

"Gotcha."

Cutting through walls and flooring, he rushed to the front room. His heart dropped. In one corner of the room, Cecily crouched, her switchblade close to her body and pointing outward as she stared at Madame Ti. Cecily could not see the details, but she had to know Madame Ti was in trouble. The witch had both her hands out, each one for a different ghost.

Madame Ti stood in her casting circle, all of her concentration working hard to hold these two ghosts in check. Locked in her left hand, she held a man with a grizzled beard and pock marks all over his skin. In her right hand, her spell had captured Mr. Derby.

Though Max had no true affection for Mr. Derby, he thought it would be easier to lend his aid by attacking the grizzled bearded man. With a spry movement, Max body-checked Grizzled Beard, pushing him through the wall. As he heard Madame Ti's relief, Grizzled Beard growled and came soaring back. Max used a simple step back and deflection move, and it still marveled him how his martial arts training had proven effective. Madame Ti whispered two words and thrust her palms forward. Mr. Derby disappeared.

Answering Max's unspoken question, she said, "He'll be back."

"If you want that finger, you and Cecily need to go upstairs and dig up the floorboards in the back corner. There's a metal tin. Open it up and bring its contents to me."

"Do-it-yourself, ghost."

"I'll have an easier time protecting my wife."

"We don't care what you —"

Grizzled Beard charged into the room like a bull in heat. His head rammed into Max's gut and the two smashed out onto the porch.

Tumbling through the air, Max threw two punches for every one he received. But his jabs and palm strikes did less damage than the punches coming from Grizzled Beard.

The ghost had a lot of bulk on him, and that created a lot of power. How ghost mass could create power without weight was a puzzle Max would have to research some other day — provided he survived, of course.

Using an elbow to the side of the head, Max dazed Grizzled Beard enough to get free. Ignoring the large ghost, Max rushed back to the house. He burst into the front room and found Madame Ti and Cecily standing over Jessica Mobley's limp form. "Get upstairs and get me that tin," Max said.

With a perturbed glower, Madame Ti said, "Patience. We're negotiating." She turned her attention back to Cecily. "Your ghost has returned. He demands the metal tin. Like I said."

Cecily slipped the knife away. "And he says with the tin he can get the finger?"

"So he says."

"Then why do we wait?"

If the lives of his wife and boys did not depend on it, Max would have found the situation amusing. Cecily Hull may have played out her plan to regain power, but she did not have that power yet. Madame Ti knew it. The witch wanted to make sure she squeezed all that Hull was worth before becoming a subordinate.

Apparently, Cecily figured it out, too. "I can do it myself then."

"Good luck," Madame Ti said. "It's a large attic. It could take you a long time to find which floorboards the tin is under. And the way the ghosts keep coming in here and attacking, I don't think you'll have that much time. Anything happens to the wife here, and you've lost all your leverage."

"I still have the boys."

"I'm not so sure." Madame Ti's words perked Max's

interest. "We never got a confirmation call from your men. If they had an accident, then those boys are either in police custody, lost in the woods, or dead."

Max did not want to think about the implications, and Grizzled Beard obliged. The bullish ghost blitzed into the room. Max punched the oncoming beast and had the satisfaction of connecting with the man's already flat nose. Had they been alive, Max would have re-broken the nose — probably for the third or fourth time — but he also would have broken his own fingers. As ghosts, they both suffered the pain but lacked the final injury.

Cecily stomped toward Madame Ti. "You should be very careful about rankling me. I have appreciation for your greed, but I also value loyalty. We went through a lot to get to this point. Turn on me now, and when this is over, you'll regret that decision."

Moving faster than expected, Grizzled Beard pivoted, reached back, and grabbed Max in a reverse headlock. Shifting his nonexistent ghost weight, he flipped Max over and followed up by planting his elbow in Max's gut. Reeling with pain, Max tried to figure out how Grizzled Beard had managed any of it. But then, Grizzled Beard circled above Sandra.

"I'm not asking for much," Madame Ti said. "It simply occurred to me that when this bloodshed is done, there won't be much left of the Magi or the Mobley coven. Instead of working directly for you, it would be beneficial to us both if I were to head up a coven of my own."

"Beneficial to you, yes. But how is this a good idea for me?" Cecily asked.

Grizzled Beard moved in closer to Sandra. He inhaled deeply as if he could smell the life in her. He ran his finger from her forehead down to her chin, tracing the features of her face like a sculptor seeking out imperfections in the stone. He winced at the pain of touching a living person.

Ignoring every signal of strain and injury, Max jetted across the short distance between him and Grizzled Beard. Leading with his knees, he bashed Grizzled Beard in the side, and the momentum sent the two of them outdoors once more.

Issuing a flurry of punches, Max advanced upon Grizzled Beard. Perhaps the old ghost could tell something had changed because he did not retaliate as before. Instead, he scurried away. But Max kept on the ghost. He would not let Grizzled Beard have a chance to recoup and return.

Grizzled Beard must have realized he could not escape. With another animalistic roar, he shot back at Max, his meaty fists landing hard more often than not. The two traded blows until Grizzled Beard managed an uppercut that sent Max's mind spinning.

Max stumbled back — as much of a stumble as a ghost could make — and tried to clear his head. He heard Grizzled Beard approaching. He tasted something in his mouth — couldn't be blood — but it couldn't be anything good, either.

And then he saw it.

On the ground. Next to the bleeding body of the Magi woman. A bracelet with two special charms attached to it. The first protected the wearer from minor magical assaults. The second — the one that interested Max the most — deflected ghosts in the same way that an invisible fence shocked a dog.

This is going to hurt.

He waited until Grizzled Beard was nearly upon him. He could feel the larger ghost hovering over and pictured that huge fist smashing down on the back of his head. He could not let it get that far. Counting in his head, he waited until his resolve would not hold him in place any longer. With one quick movement, Max snatched the bracelet from the ground, screamed at the electric pain ripping through him, and locked the bracelet around Grizzled Beard's wrist. The fist connected with Max's chest. Max flew back. But the bracelet remained behind.

As Grizzled Beard whimpered, the old ghost scurried around, screaming and crying as if he had banged his wrist in a car door but unable to think clear enough about where the pain came from and what to do about it. Max had no sympathy. His mind stayed focused on saving Sandra and the boys.

When he got back to the house, Madame Ti and Cecily still debated.

"As long as you and your new coven members will swear a blood allegiance to the Hull family as led by me or a chosen successor, then it is agreed. Provided you also acknowledge that we are not equals. The Hull family will be the ruling body of magic in all of North Carolina, and you will help me spread that influence beyond."

Madame Ti nodded. "The metal tin is in the back corner alcove."

Cecily took one long stride putting her nose to nose with Madame Ti. "You expect me to dig around in the dirt and filth upstairs?"

"I'll be happy to do it for you, but then you'll have to prepare the spell down here so that I can bring Crutchfield back using whatever is in that tin. Can you do that?"

From the look on Cecily's face, Max worried she had been pushed too far. It would take little to send Cecily into a blind rage — not only because of Madame Ti's greedy renegotiation, but the simple matter of the adrenaline pumping through her from being in a war zone. And Cecily Hull was armed — twice over. Her gun still had ammunition and the stiletto never ran out.

Max wanted to intervene but short of chilling bones and freezing brains, he did not know what his ghost-body was capable of.

Bounding off toward the ladder, Cecily said, "That spell better be ready when I get back."

A few moments later, sounds of stomping around upstairs and floorboards being ripped open reached down below. Dust and dirt sprinkled through the ceiling. Madame Ti knelt on a clean part of the floor and began a new casting circle. Max settled next to his wife, wishing he could hold her hand or stroke her hair. At least, she could hear him. Or so he hoped.

"Hang in there, honey. We're doing everything we can to bring you back. And I'm sorry for — well, for not delivering on the promise of our marriage. Seems to me that part of my job as your husband was to help provide a stable life. I don't mean that we had to be rich or successful or any of that. But the least you should have been able to expect from me was a roof over our heads. And I know, I know — it's not just the man's job to do these things. We're a team. We've always worked best as a team. But, if you'll permit me to be brutally honest — and let's face it, in your current condition, you can't really argue — the truth is that in any marriage the roles get divvied up. It may not be traditional, of course. Maybe the wife goes off to work and makes all the money while the husband stays home and raises the kids. That's okay. Maybe they both go off to make money and a nanny raises the kids. Maybe there are no kids. The point is that we have our roles to play. Ever since you and I moved in with my mother, our roles have been all over the place. You and I have been jumping on top of each other trying to keep above water, but in doing so, it's like were shoving the other one under. I know we worked a bit of this out, but I want you to hear me, come back to me, understand that I'm holding out my hand to you. So, here's my promise. You hang in there. Don't give up on me. You come back, and we'll find a way to bring me back, too. And then, I promise, we'll straighten our lives out. We'll figure out whose job is what, especially when it comes to raising our boys, and we'll start living our life again instead of just treading water. I love you too much to let something like a witch's spell and curse stop us." He blew a kiss towards her.

Before he could say more, Cecily returned holding the grimy tin. She popped the top off and handed it out toward Madame Ti. The witch stepped over and glanced inside. She lifted a chain necklace with a gold locket. Madame Ti ran her finger along the locket and then flicked it open.

"Interesting," she said. Max flew behind to peek over her shoulder. The two portraits inside the locket were of a handsome black man on the left and a young child on the right. Though he could not guarantee it, Max suspected this was the family of Mary Goins.

"Will it work?" Cecily asked.

Madame Ti took the locket over to the casting circle. "Provided this truly belonged to William Crutchfield — or at least, it held significance to him — it'll work."

For the next several minutes, nobody spoke. Madame Ti stood before the circle and drew the strange symbol that Sandra had been researching. She closed her eyes and opened her arms wide like some Aztec priestess preparing for a sacrifice.

Max felt a shift in the air as if the entire house had changed altitude. The pleasant aroma of burning wood drifted through the room. This juxtaposition of pleasant and unsettling twisted within Max leaving him wary of what might come. His distrust for the witch led his mind down several dark and disturbing possibilities.

Madame Ti slapped the air above the circle. A flash of light. An electric sizzle.

Crutchfield, locked in Drummond's bear hug, flew through the window.

"Got him," Drummond said. Crutchfield wrenched one direction and then the other. He kicked up and smacked his head back at Drummond.

Madame Ti swiped the necklace off the floor and held it before Crutchfield. He thrashed about like a madman attempting to evade the straitjacket. Until he saw the locket.

He ceased. His head dropped. Drummond relaxed his hold on the ghost, and Crutchfield showed no sign of attempting escape.

"I think he's ready to behave civilly," Madame Ti said.

"How about it?" Drummond said. "You ready to listen to us?"

"No," Crutchfield said. "You need to listen to me."

Chapter 27

DRUMMOND POKED CRUTCHFIELD in the collarbone. "Look, pal, you are not in any position to make demands on who should be listening to who. We've gone through a hell of a lot to get you here. It's time for you to help us out. You want to resist? Fine by me. I've started to enjoy punching you."

"If y'all will just listen to me," Crutchfield said raising his hands, "I think you'll find we can help each other."

"Really? I thought we were servants of the devil. Why would you want to help us?"

"I don't want to help you. I want to help them."

Max followed Crutchfield's gaze outside. Drifting towards the entranceway, Max saw them — all the ghosts encircled the house. Sick Girl, Mr. Derby, portly woman — every single one of them hovered, watched, and waited. An odd quiet developed around them, and Max wondered if the battle had ended or if some magic had created the lack of sound.

"What is it about that locket?" Max said. "Will that help the ghosts outside?"

Still holding the locket, Madame Ti said, "Stand in the circle and be seen. Stand in the circle and be heard. Deny me and I shall banish you, never to be seen or heard again."

Drummond said, "Sheesh, this one doesn't mess around."

Crutchfield floated into the circle, and by their reactions, clearly Madame Ti and Cecily could now see him. Max glanced outside once more. He could not imagine the pest house ghosts would wait too long. He tried to gain Sick Girl's attention but she refused to look at him. Mr. Derby was no better.

Like a participant in a hypnosis act, Crutchfield watched the pendant dangling from Madame Ti's hand. On the verge of tears that his ghostly existence could not produce, he clasped his hands in front of him and bowed his head. He rubbed his fingers, and Max noticed a dark layer of grime underneath his nails. He did not know why, but Max thought this lent authenticity to Crutchfield's words.

"My mother was a very superstitious woman."

"We do not need your entire life story," Cecily said.

"Be quiet, woman. You're no witch, so you have no power over me."

Madame Ti said, "I am a witch, and she is my employer."

Crutchfield looked to Drummond and received a solemn nod. Shaking his head in disbelief, Crutchfield said, "Witches broke into the house one night, tied me up, drew a casting circle, and outright killed my mother. Didn't even bother with a curse. Just used magic in a way that would look like a heart attack."

"So you became a witch hunter," Max said.

"Spent my whole life hunting down witches. Killed them all throughout the South and much of the North, too. Killed minor witches, major ones, weak ones, powerful ones, and even ones who had no idea what they'd gotten themselves into. Killed them all."

Cecily said, "Get to the point."

Drummond nodded. "I hate to agree with her, but people are dying out there. And he's been stuck in this building for over a hundred years. If we're not careful, he's going to break out a game of Jenga."

In a soothing tone that Max hoped did not sound

patronizing, he said, "What happened with Mary Goins? We read the court records, but what happened that's not in the official story?"

Throwing a dirty look their way, Crutchfield said, "I had never killed a civilian. Those I killed were monsters, and it felt no different than killing a deer or a rabid dog. Just a beast that needed killing. But Mary Goins — well, I never gave her the chance to make that decision. It destroyed me."

"If you felt so bad, why did it take you so many years to confess to her murder?"

"Mister, I'll tell you this — guilt and shame can make a man behave in strange ways. I spent several years traveling across the country, discovering the floors of many bars and houses of ill repute. I tried to wash off the stain of sin with more sin. But no matter how much I drunk, no matter how much debauchery I partook in, the last thing I would see before I fell asleep was the face of Mary Goins. It was a curse of my own making. Serves me right that on my travels back here for redemption, I got sick."

"The pest house. You checked yourself in."

"That I did. I hoped I could stay here quietly, get better, and hunt down Mobley and Hope."

"Because they wanted Mary Goins?"

"The whole mess was their fault."

Pacing around the casting circle, Drummond moved like an interrogating officer. "Hold on there. Are you telling me that all those ghosts outside ready to come in here and rip everybody to shreds, they're all cursed because you felt guilty about being a witch hunter? You're saying you came out here to get rid of two powerful witches but cowered out and hid amongst these people who were dying anyway? Is that about right?"

"I didn't say it was fair."

"You listen to me. I was cursed for almost a hundred years. Not as long as you, but long enough. I don't really care what your sob story is, I want you to give us one of your fingers so we can be done with all of this."

"I will not give you so much as a thumb until my demands are met."

Before Drummond could launch into the circle with a punch, Max glided forward. "Everyone calm down." Although Cecily could not directly hear Max, she had the intelligence to observe in silence. For the moment. "I understand the need to set things right. It's all about restoring a sense of balance to the world. There's always going to be good and evil. We know that. We serve nobody if we lie to ourselves and pretend that good can prevail at all times. Evil gets its day now and then. But we are the light in the darkness. We are the ones who fight back so that evil does not take over. We are the force to create balance and stability in our world.

"Y'know, not too long ago, I felt like you must have felt before you got cursed. What was the point? Why go through all this trouble if you're just going to end up dying in some cot in some attic out in the middle of nowhere? I get it. I do. Because you know that no matter how many witches you kill, there's always going to be another. There's always going to be a woman like Mary Goins who has the power within her to become a strong and dangerous witch. But unlike Mary, there are women who *will* be seduced by that power. And the witches keep coming. No matter how many witch hunters are out there, no matter how many paranormal investigators, no matter how many people willing to fight the supernatural, the monsters still come. So what does it all matter?"

Drummond said, "You might want to get to the point soon because right now you're making a real good case for him to never help us."

One look at Crutchfield and Max knew he had gotten through to the man. Crutchfield stroked his mustache with a thoughtful motion. Max went on, "Here's the thing — and you'll want to listen to this part because it's the part you've been missing. It's the part I'm only starting to see myself. Just like there are people out there who are drawn to the evil, who are seduced by its power, there are also other people who are drawn to fight. That's you. And me and Drummond and my wife. If we don't hold up our end of things, then evil prevails. If we don't answer the call, the challenge, then evil prevails. There's a huge world out there, and I'm only fighting witches in a small part of North Carolina. For crying out loud, there's got to be a lot of other witch hunters out there. There has to be. If there weren't, the whole world would have succumbed to evil a long time ago.

"That's it. That's all I have to offer. We need you to give us one of your fingers, so that my wife and my boys are not harmed. So that we can do our job and find a balance to all of this horribly wrong crap."

Crutchfield pointed at Madame Ti. "She's going to take the finger from you. She's going to use it to spread evil. Both of them will."

"Probably," Max said, the admission choking off in his throat.

Cecily stepped up next to Madame Ti. "We are not evil. We want to bring order to the chaos that's been going on. Nobody is in charge of the witches right now. For a long time, my family did keep a tight rein on them. That's all I'm trying to do."

With a sneer, Crutchfield said, "I know exactly what your kind wants."

Max said, "I know it hurts. I know it feels like losing.

Believe me, it makes me sick to my stomach having to work with these people. But I promise you this. No matter what happens tonight, I will do everything I can to stop them from achieving their goals. I am not giving up. I don't care if I'm a half-ghost for all of eternity, I will grab hold of that light and be part of the balancing weight in this world. What about you? You're still here. You haven't moved on yet. You can still do good."

Crutchfield appeared to weigh Max's words. He dropped his arms to his sides and the hardest look Max had ever seen on anybody's face overcame Crutchfield's features. He said, "You can have my finger."

Cecily clicked her teeth. "It's about time."

Raising a hand to stop the celebration, Crutchfield went on, "You can have the finger, and in exchange, your witch has to break the curse upon all the ghosts stuck to this house."

Madame Ti said, "You want me to break a curse formed by both Mother Hope and Grandma Mobley? Impossible."

"Not impossible. If you're as powerful as I hear — and frankly, I can feel the power coming off of you — then it is within your ability to break that curse. You only have to be willing to make the right sacrifices."

Madame Ti paled as she turned toward Cecily. Max did not have to see their faces to know what transpired between them. The sacrifice could only mean one thing — one of Madame Ti's eyes. A witch's eye, in conjunction with a casting triangle, created powerful magic. Extremely powerful. Cecily expected Madame Ti to agree. But, of course, Madame Ti would not be keen to lose an eye.

Perhaps sensing that she could not take the conversation into a private room, not without risking Crutchfield's escape, Madame Ti said, "If I agree to this, then I want more than simply my own coven."

Cecily crossed her arms and with a respectful grin, she said, "I'm listening."

"Once I establish my coven, I want all others in the state to answer to mine. Think of my coven as the Coven of Covens and I will be its Queen. No witch will be permitted to even sneeze without my say-so."

"And will you still be answerable to me?"

"I can agree to that." Madame Ti raised her index finger. "On one condition. If I do this, if I pluck out my eye, then one day, I can call upon you to make a sacrifice for me."

Cecily frowned. "What kind of sacrifice? Will you expect me to pluck out my own eye, too?"

"What would I want with your eye? Consider it a grand favor that you owe me. A marker that I can call in when I need it. Because we both know what this world is like, and there will come a time that I will need your help when it may not be convenient to you. I need your word that you will be there when I call."

"That's it? You want my word?"

Max opened his mouth to clarify things for Cecily, but Drummond stopped him with a sharp push on the shoulder. To give one's word to a witch meant more than a blood-oath or a promise written in stone. Should Cecily agree and willfully give her word, she would never be able to break it. Not without serious consequences. Ones that made Max's curse look pedestrian.

Cecily said, "Fine, fine. You have my word."

Madame Ti turned back to Crutchfield. Looking green, she said, "Very well. Give us your finger, and I will break the curse upon the ghosts. Betray me and I will see that every last one of them suffers a far worse fate than they already undergo."

Crutchfield said, "No need for threats. Let's get this on with."

Chapter 28

FOR A WOMAN WHO HAD JUST AGREED to remove her own eye, Madame Ti showed remarkable poise. With barely a hint of shaking in her hand, she drew a new circle on the floor. She did, however, flinch at the grating of chalk against wood.

Only a few feet away, Jessica Mobley remained unconscious. Max worried his inexperience with freezing brains may have caused more damage than simply knocking her out. Drummond did not share his concern, but then Drummond may not have cared too greatly since Jessica was a witch.

Madame Ti finished drawing the symbols around the circle and knelt fully inside it. "I need the finger to be placed in the circle with me."

Crutchfield peered out at the ghosts circling the house before grabbing his ring finger on his left hand. With a quick motion, the finger flopped backward. Max never heard a snap — but then why would he? There was no bone to break. In fact, the more Max thought about it, the more he wondered what Crutchfield actually had done to remove his finger.

"Don't be fooled," Drummond said, speaking low so only Max would hear him. "He might not have any bones in his body, but that's got to hurt something awful."

Max could see it on Crutchfield's face. The ghost did his best to hide any reaction, but he clearly suffered through the process. If a ghost could sweat, Crutchfield's brow would have beaded up fast.

Holding the pale finger out, Crutchfield waited. Drummond drifted over, picked up the finger, and delivered it to Madame Ti's casting circle. She paused. The slim appendage hung before her and, whether on purpose or not, Drummond had the finger pointing at her. Max held back a chuckle — definitely on purpose. Madame Ti stared at the finger as if she had expected — or hoped — that Crutchfield would renege on the deal and in doing so, save her from losing her eye. But the ghostly finger lowered to the casting circle and lay like a shriveled worm.

With tight lips, she closed her eyes and worked at her spell. A few minutes went by, and then a puff of smoke rose from the finger.

Max looked to Drummond. "You think that's it?"

Madame Ti stood and took one large step backwards. She then knelt and drew a triangle. She adorned its sides with new symbols — symbols with thicker lines and more jagged shapes. Like carrying a cup of water in the desert, she carefully scooped the finger between her hands and slowly walked it over to the triangle. When she set it in place, she rubbed her hands vigorously against each other. Though the finger had taken on enough solidity to be transferred by a human, clearly it still clung to its ghostly cold.

Continuing her preparations for the final stage of the spell, she dashed off several more symbols. Max had a moment of awe at the accomplished level of witchcraft the woman possessed. When Sandra had to cast a spell, she often spent time consulting books and double-checking her symbols before writing them down. But like Mother Hope and Grandma Mobley, Madame Ti appeared to have the knowledge at her fingertips.

Mother Hope. Max recalled the way her small form felt in his hands as she spoke her dying words. Like holding a bird — a brittle weight that might be crushed if he was careless. He had asked to be freed from this curse and she told him to get the finger and give it to Cecily Hull. At the time, he thought she made a poor joke. But witches rarely wasted words. And on her deathbed? Max couldn't imagine she would waste a single syllable. So, why would she say that?

Madame Ti twisted to the side and put out her hand toward Cecily. "Your blade."

Snapping out the switchblade, Cecily placed the weapon in Madame Ti's hand. With all the reverence given to a ceremonial dagger, the witch brought the blade into the triangle and set it next to the finger. It clinked as it touched the floor — twice — because her shaking hands could not set it firmly enough.

Drummond drifted over to Max once more. "What's wrong?"

"Nothing," Max said.

"I know that look on your face. Something is troubling you."

"I'm just trying to figure out something Mother Hope had said."

After a cleansing breath, Madame Ti wiped her hands on her thighs. She reached forward and lifted the switchblade. Wrapping her fingers around the grip, she raised it high above her, looked up at it, and pointed the blade toward her awaiting eye. "For all that gives me power, for the Earth and the natural world that thrives upon it, for tomorrow's victories, I make this sacrifice."

If she had prepared a spell to numb the pain, Max had not seen it happen. But she brought the blade down without hesitation. It slammed into her eye socket. Cecily gasped and covered her mouth. Max cringed. Even Drummond and Crutchfield recoiled. With the swift, well-practiced motions of a butcher, Madame Ti severed her eye and scooped it out, letting it drop into the center of the triangle. Max did his best to forget the wet sound of it hitting the floor.

All remained still.

Madame Ti rolled her shoulders back and dropped the knife. It clattered on the floor — the noise drowned out by the enormous wailing of the witch. Blood streamed down the side of her face as her hands clenched the sky above her. She howled like an angry wolf.

Despite all her thundering distress, Max could see the corners of her mouth. They curved upward. He had seen that mad smile before — on Mother Hope's face. Right before she died, as she told Max to get the finger and give it to Cecily, Mother Hope's mouth had skirted the edge of a grin.

Deep, gasping breaths shook Madame Ti's body as she returned to her more controlled self. With two fingers, she dabbed at the open wound on her face. She took a dollop of blood and touched one corner of the triangle. "For magic."

Max wondered — what if Mother Hope had retained a slice of her humanity right before she died? Perhaps she told Max to get that finger because it could help him be free of the curse.

Madame Ti touched the second corner of the triangle. "For nature."

No. Mother Hope had said her final words with vindictive pride. This whole spell of Madame Ti's had one purpose. To take that finger and return it to full flesh. Exactly the same thing Max wanted for himself.

Madame Ti touched the final corner. "For Earth."

Not only was the spell supposed to bring the finger into the corporeal world, but Madame Ti had cut out her eye to give her the strength to break Mother Hope and Grandma Mobley's curse. If Mother Hope wanted this to happen, then she must have expected something else to occur. Perhaps ... Could it be that simple? Could he use the spell, too?

Drummond started to speak, but Max waved him off and drifted closer. He watched Madame Ti like a skeptic watching the deft maneuvers of a sleight-of-hand artist. He had to time things right.

Before he could think through it further, Madame Ti raised her bloodied hand. He knew she would bring it down upon the writing on the floor and the spell would go off. It was all happening at this moment. No time to weigh out the choices.

His gut told him to go for it. As Madame Ti brought her hand down, Max shot forward. When the hand hit the floor, he leapt into the triangle.

Chapter 29

MAX JOLTED UPRIGHT. In the attic. In his body.

His heart pounded in his chest — and he could feel it. He could feel the rhythm of his heart pumping blood through his body. Peering down, he could see his chest rise and fall with each breath. His mouth tasted dry and dusty.

He brought his hand to his lips and prodded his fingers with the tip of his tongue. Salty, dirty, and wonderful. He fell back, his mouth open wide, and the glory of his body hitting the wooden floor and not falling through became a momentary religious experience. He glimpsed what some followers must feel at a church revival or a gospel service — that overwhelming emotion which forced one to jump in the aisle dancing or fall to the ground weeping. He was alive, whole, returned from the fate he thought he would never escape.

He felt something in his other hand. Sitting up, he opened his fingers to find an extra finger — William Crutchfield's made whole. He remembered — he grabbed it just as Madame Ti's spell went off.

It worked. The spell made them both whole. The spell had destroyed Mother Hope's curse upon him.

Looking to his right, he saw Grandma Mobley's clothes and a layer of dust that had once been her body. Such a waste. All those years spent trying to manipulate people and control outcomes, all those years building her power base, and in the end, reduced to a pile of hate-filled ashes.

Rising to his feet, Max attempted to walk to the ladder. He weaved and his head had trouble staying straight up.

Like being intoxicated. Like the results of too many punches to the head. But he pushed onward. He paused only when he reached Mother Hope.

She moved. A little, but a clear movement. With a grunt, she pushed up onto her elbows. With a dazed look, she said, "Thank you."

"You knew I'd do this? That I'd jump into that spell?"

"I believe they call it a Hail Mary. I couldn't know for sure what you would do, but it was the only move I had left. Besides, I always win."

Max's newly pounding heart dropped. This horrible evil had returned and what could he do?

She coughed. Then she coughed again. Her brow tightened. "Something's not right."

Her skin turned sandy brown and her eyes snapped open wide. "Madame Ti," she whispered as her lips flaked off. In seconds, she disintegrated. Less than the ash that had been Grandma Mobley, all that stayed behind of Mother Hope was her clothing.

Max watched the pile of clothes until he felt certain that she was finally gone. He put his hand on the top rung of the ladder and swung his leg down. The momentum brought him around too fast. The world spun and he dropped through the air. His foot caught on one rung and banged on another. His arms clobbered against the wood. The rung broke free and he tumbled. When he hit the floor, the wind rushed from his lungs but nothing broke. His befuddled state must have relaxed his body enough that he flopped down like a rag doll.

Drummond rushed into the room. "Look at you." He clapped his hands together once. "When I saw you jump into that spell, I thought that was the last time I'd ever see you. That may have been the craziest thing I've ever witnessed. Pretty stupid, too."

Groaning as he pushed himself back to a sitting position, Max said, "It worked. Mother Hope gave me the idea."

"Yeah? I wouldn't question it. I learned long ago to take a win when you get one. We still have enough problems not to turn our noses up at a good moment like this. I'm glad you're okay. I'm glad you're back."

"Got a bonus, too." Max held up Crutchfield's finger.

"Well, I'll be."

A disorienting wave rolled up from his stomach and spread over his head. Bile raced up his throat, and as he swallowed it down, the bitter taste and acidic burn had never been so pleasant. He was alive. And even the less desirable parts of that statement brought him joy. For the moment.

"Come on," Drummond said. "We still have work to do."

Bumbling through the house, bumping door jambs and weaving into walls, Max made his way toward the front of the house. Long before he reached them, he heard Cecily's clipped tones as she berated Madame Ti for failure.

Stepping into the room, he saw Madame Ti wrapping a cloth around her head to cover her eye. No mistaking the simmering anger on her face. He said, "Though I love hearing you lay into that witch, I've got to tell you that she succeeded." He held up Crutchfield's finger.

"I see," Cecily said, her anger shifting to greedy excitement. "Hand it over. We had a deal."

Max closed his fist around the finger. "You have another deal, too. One you made with Crutchfield."

"I have full faith that Madame Ti has fulfilled our end of that bargain."

Max turned towards Drummond, using most of his strength to keep from falling over.

"Stay standing," Drummond said. "I'll check it out."

The few seconds his partner needed to float outside and return with news stretched into an eternity. The urge to curl up next to Sandra and close his eyes kept singing to him. It would be simple. And pleasurable, too. But Max gave his head a quick shake and attempted to refocus. There would be time to sleep later.

Drummond reappeared in the doorway. "She told the truth. The ghosts are all free. Most are rushing into the woods to find where their bodies were buried."

Still in the casting circle so that all could see him, Crutchfield bowed his head. "Thank you. You did an honorable thing today."

Cecily said, "Perhaps this will prove to you that I have good intentions with the way the Hull family will guide witchcraft in the future."

"Plenty of evil has been borne from good intentions. But if you continue to do good, I'll have no quarrel. If not, then you'll be seeing me again. You won't like that."

Crutchfield spent the time to lock eyes with every person in the room. Max got the message — Crutchfield's words were not meant solely for Cecily Hull. When he finished holding his threatening gaze with Drummond, the ghost gave his mustache one final grooming stroke and slipped away from view.

Max said to Drummond, "Did he just move on?"

"He went outside. He's talking with a few ghosts that stuck around. Given everything we know about him, I can't say whether he'll get to move on or not. On the one hand, he did a lot of good to protect people from evil. On the other hand, witches or not, he murdered a lot of women. And you know, the rules about the whole moving on thing aren't made that much clearer once you get where I am. I guess we'll just have to wait and see."

Cecily Hull put out her hand. "You see that I honored my end of the deal. Your turn now. Hand over the finger."

Before Max could step toward Cecily, Drummond blocked him with an arm. "Something's happening here."

Max held back. "What's wrong?"

"Nothing," Cecily said. "Give me Crutchfield's finger."

"I wasn't talking to you."

Drummond said, "One of the ghosts came in. A young girl. She looks very angry."

Sick Girl. "What's she doing?" Not being able to see her anymore left Max with a queasy crawl along his skin.

Madame Ti dropped to the floor as Drummond said, "She swiped her hand through the witch's head. That's it. She's gone."

It took Madame Ti a few seconds to regain consciousness, but she got back on her feet. "I suppose that would be under the heading of no good deed goes unpunished." Letting her gaze envelope the room, she added, "You listen to me, ghost. I killed Mother Hope. Don't think I can't get to you."

Tapping her foot, Cecily wiggled the fingers of her open hand. "Don't make me ask again."

"Stop." The voice chilled Max's skin — not only because of its fierce command but because of where it came from. Behind him.

Sandra rose from the couch. She did not stumble. She did not sway. With her hands out as if ready to cast a spell, she stood firm and tall with her eyes concentrating on Madame Ti.

Drummond tipped back his hat. "Huh. Looks like that girl did us a little favor."

Indeed. When Sick Girl attacked Madame Ti, she knocked the witch unconscious for a few precious seconds. Max had not realized it at the time, but it was clear now —

Madame Ti needed to be conscious in order to maintain her control over Sandra's state. Earlier, when Sick Girl dazed Madame Ti with a blow of wood to the head, Sandra stirred. Max wondered if Sick Girl understood then what needed to be done. He grinned. *Thank you, Sick Girl.*

Max rushed over and scooped Sandra up into a tight hug. Tears rolled down his cheeks as he kissed her hair. But she wriggled free and stepped away. He could see it on her face — she wanted to fold into his arms, but there would be time for affection later. They still had to survive the next few minutes.

"Our boys," Sandra said, glowering at Cecily. "The deal was that Max would get you the finger in exchange for our boys."

Max turned back. "That's right. And I know for a fact that you have not heard from the men who took PB and J."

"I'm sure they are fine," Cecily said, looking anything but sure.

"Once we can confirm —"

"Enough of this," Madame Ti said as she approached.

Sandra pushed in front of Max and raised her hands. "When it comes to those boys, you do not want to mess with me."

"Oh, come now. We both know that you can't —"

A deluge of energy lashed out of Sandra's hands. It knocked Madame Ti back several steps until she pressed up against the far wall. Cecily inched away, her eyes wide and concerned.

Sandra said, "Just because you had me unconscious doesn't mean I was asleep. I couldn't get myself to fully awaken, but I was aware of — well, some things, anyway."

Drummond snickered. "Doll, you're one of the greatest. Using all that time to prep up a spell so it was ready to go off at a moment's notice. I love it."

Max said, "We want our boys. Sandra has had plenty of time to store up quite a few spells. You don't want to test that." He had no clue if Sandra had the skill to hold more than one spell at a time, but he guessed his confidence would cause Madame Ti and Cecily a second thought.

"Hold on, hold on," Drummond said. "Call Irene Beck. She was supposed to come here to pick up the boys so that you wouldn't have to worry about them. But I was too late getting to her. She should have arrived, though. There's only one road in and out of here, so it's possible that she knows what happened to them. Maybe she saw them being taken away and decided to follow. Maybe she had a gunfight with them. We didn't hear anything, but it was hard to hear much over the battle. I don't know, but it's strange that she didn't call you."

Max checked his phone. No messages. He called Irene, and in a few short moments, he had the most wonderful answers to share with Sandra. "The boys are safe," Max said. "She was coming up the road to pick them up when Cecily's thugs came the other way. She says she sensed the boys were in there and in trouble. You're not going to believe this part — she ran them off the road."

"I believe it," Drummond said. "There's a reason I like that gal."

"Anyway, the boys jumped in the car with her, and they took off. She didn't call us because she didn't know if we were compromised in any way. She figured we would call her when everything was okay or that she'd hear from Drummond."

Keeping her eyes on Madame Ti, Sandra's voice tightened. "For real, hon? The boys are okay?"

Max placed a hand on her shoulder. "They're just fine. You can let the witch go."

Sandra dropped her hands, releasing Madame Ti.

Nestling her face in Max's chest, Sandra shuddered. He had never felt so wonderful holding her at that moment. Both of them were alive, the boys were okay — his mind whirled high. They had survived. He had Sandra in his arms, and that was all that mattered.

Cecily Hull shattered that illusion. "Now that we have dispensed with all of your objections and stalling, hand over the finger or we'll test how strong your witch is against mine."

Max stepped away from Sandra, gave her a quick wink, and turned to Cecily. He handed over the finger. "I wasn't stalling. Merely trying to make sure you lived up to your end of the bargain."

"You and Crutchfield and, I imagine everybody else, must understand that things have changed. There is a new order around here. My name is Hull but I am not one of the men who came before me. When I give my word, it will be followed through on. It will never be broken."

"Good to know. How about you give me your word that you will never use witchcraft to hurt anybody?"

With a malicious grin, Cecily handed the finger to Madame Ti. "You have caused too much damage over the years and I have to fix it. I've learned that sometimes you have to break things a little before you can fix them properly. But I will give my word on this — the days of warring covens and *ad hoc* witch hunters is over. There will be a few rough weeks coming ahead, yet once the word is made clear that I am in charge, we should have a nice, stable environment where witchcraft is not going to be tossed about without care."

"I can't tell if that's a threat or a promise."

With a playful shrug, Cecily said, "Maybe a little of both."

Max didn't think Cecily would be as tough a Hull as she

thought of herself, and that left him wondering if they had traded one power vacuum for another. Then again, Madame Ti might be tough enough to take that spot.

As Cecily left, Madame Ti moved in front of Sandra. She thrust out her fist and Sandra jumped back. Madame Ti smirked.

"I guess you didn't have any spells waiting."

Sandra shrugged. "A bluff only works when the other person is willing to believe. Guess you have an idea of how dangerous I could be, if you were that afraid."

Madame Ti shook her head like a teacher knowing her student had a hard road ahead. "You better be nice to me. After all, I am going to be the Queen of Covens." She followed Cecily outside.

Max put his hand out toward his lovely wife. "I guess that means —"

Sandra took hold of Max's wrist and pulled him close. Their lips pressed tight and their arms held tighter. Not even Drummond's complaining could make Max leave that warm embrace.

Chapter 30

WHILE THEY WAITED FOR IRENE to return with the boys, Max, Sandra, and Drummond moved about the battlefield to help those who had survived. The red smoke had drifted away and dawn approached. With this new view, Max saw how small the cleared area around the house had actually been.

The ground had been turned up from trampling feet, and in many places blood had soaked the clay into a muddy brown mixture. Many of the bodies had been removed — the Magi and Mobleys cared for their own both in an effort to properly bury their dead but also to avoid leaving evidence that would trace back to them. The air smelled of burnt wood. Max's nostrils stung from another scent — a bitter odor like old oil. He guessed it was the stench of numerous magic spells going off in such a short period of time. Either that or somebody's car needed a serious tune-up.

Near the embers of the Mobley fire, Sandra helped an older coven sister to her feet. Max had never been more proud or more terrified when he saw Sandra take on Madame Ti. But the tenderness she displayed helping the Mobley witch back to her car gave him every confidence in her strength of will. He had doubted her many times when it came to her studies in witchcraft, but nothing in him worried for her anymore. She might be the only good witch in the entire world, but that was okay with him. After all, she was his wife.

"What have you got to smile about?" Lena Mobley said

as she staggered towards Max.

"Your war is over and nobody won. I think that's a victory for me."

"Cecily Hull won. Smart woman. I saw her leave just a little bit ago. She made sure I saw her. She wanted me to know who is in charge now. Did a smart thing playing us against each other. Now, the coven is gone. Jessica, myself, and Rachel over there — we're all that remain."

"You could take a lesson from all of this. Consider it the final bit of wisdom Grandma Mobley could ever give you."

"And that is?"

"You witches love to hold grudges. Love to hold power over people for the slightest infraction against you. That's what happened here and it destroyed you. The Magi, too. Grandma Mobley and Mother Hope could not forgive each other for whatever problems they've had over the last century. Their lust for power and their inflexibility led to this past night. Cecily Hull merely lit the fuse, but you witches built up all the combustibles long, long before."

"Are you suggesting I turn my back on who I am? Walk away from being a witch?"

"Not at all." Max would have liked that but he held no illusion that such a thing was possible. "I'm merely suggesting that nobody needs to ever fight like this again. A lot of lives were wasted here, and even if you had won, what would you have gained? Your coven had a nice little home in a small part of the world carved out for you to live in — now, it's an empty house for empty lives. You had the freedom to move about and live the way you wanted. Isn't that what everybody wants? Why do you have to have more? Why can't you simply let the other witches have their space?"

A thin line of blood dribbled down from underneath her hair. "I don't expect you to understand us. But I won't give up. There are three of us in this coven, and that's plenty to start building again. Witches never stay down."

Max snorted. "Don't I know it."

Lena shuffled on her feet before digging into her pocket. "Before we came out here, Grandma Mobley prepared me for the possibility that she might die." Lena pulled out an old, brass key. "She told me that in the event of her death, no matter the outcome of the battle, I was to give you this key — provided you survived, too."

"What's it open?" Max said, clasping his hands behind his back as if that would protect him from accidentally touching it.

Lena shook her head. "No idea. I was curious, but I knew enough not to ask. I hoped you would recognize it, but since you don't, the best I can guess is that Grandma Mobley either wanted you to have it for safekeeping or she thought that when the time came, you'd understand."

Lena pushed the key towards Max, but he stepped back.

"Oh, come now. It's not going to curse you."

"Why should I believe that?"

Lena tossed the key and hit Max in the chest — right next to the spot where Mother Hope had cursed him. The key fell to the ground with a dull thump.

"See? You're fine." With a dismissive wave, she headed towards the cars. "I hope not to see you again."

"That makes two of us." As Max snatched the key off the ground, he suspected it was only wishful thinking. He pocketed the key as he walked on. Every muscle complained and he wondered how many hours under a hot shower would be required to ease the pain.

A gruff voice called out, "I'm glad your aches didn't transfer to me."

Max squinted up into the headlights of a sedan. Leon Moore leaned against the door. With a sigh, Max said,

"Happy to see you're alive."

"Really? Didn't seem like a thing you cared about."

"That linking curse was a matter of survival. I never thought she'd actually use it if it meant hurting you."

Leon chuckled to himself. "You Porters are quite a load of garbage. You profess that you're the fighters of witches, yet you use witchcraft all the time. You say you never intended for me to be hurt, yet you put me directly in the crosshairs of a curse."

"I'm sorry about that. I only —"

"Shut up. I don't care. The fact is that however you managed to break the curse, you also broke it for me."

"We were linked."

"I only came back out here to help my fellow Magi. With Mother Hope gone, things might get a little dicey. But I've already spoken with Annie. I think the two of us will be able to hold the organization together just fine." He opened his car door. "You can let all your witch friends know that the Magi are not going away. And since its leaders are no longer going to be witches, we don't have a soft spot for them. In other words, you can let all the Mobleys and Madames out there know that it'll soon be open season on their sorry asses."

Leon drove away. When the last of the survivors also drove off, a blue town car rolled up in the opposite direction. The left front corner had a large dent in it from where Irene rammed the truck of the boys' kidnappers. Before the car stopped completely, the doors flew open and PB and J sprinted for Sandra. Max jogged towards them. The view of his wife and boys blurred, and he rubbed his eyes. They broke away only enough to make room for him to join in.

PB rattled off the excitement of Irene saving them while J simply pressed harder against Sandra. Max knew he wore a goofy grin, but he didn't care. Part of him wanted to hold that grin forever. Make it the foundation of all future grins.

"Hate to break up the joyful moment," Drummond said, "but there was a reason everybody cleaned up and left. At some point, the police are going to be here."

"Right," Max said. "Time to get out of here."

Chapter 31

IT TOOK THEM TWO MONTHS to find a good house, but they had finally succeeded. Just a starter home to the northeast of the city, right off Reidsville Road — a small, two bedroom place with a kitchen and living room, only one bathroom and a one-car garage. As the boys helped lug in the few boxes they had, Max put his arm around Sandra, and they stared at their new beginning. "Once we get our finances settled — especially once we figured out how much having two boys will cost us on a regular basis — we can start building from there."

"You sure this is okay?" Ever since they put a down payment on the home, Sandra had been concerned that their previous disagreements had pressured Max too much.

"It's not ideal, but you can miss your whole life waiting around for things to be ideal."

PB walked over carrying a large brown box marked STUDY. "Where does this go?"

Max said, "In the kitchen. I'm going to take the back corner near the pantry and set up my home office there." If anything, that was the room he would miss most from their old house. Having his own study had filled him with a weird pride. It shouldn't have, though. He continually reminded himself that having a room to work in was nothing more than that — a place to work. They had the Porter Agency office, too. No real need for anything else. Besides, after spending several months of his life cramped in his mother's apartment, he considered any space larger than a coat closet to be an improvement.

Max's mother had opted not to join them for the move in. Probably would not be coming over for a dinner anytime soon either. As far as she knew, the night of the witch battle was a night of drinking and partying that Max and Sandra did not return from until the following day. Mrs. Porter would be angry with them and their parenting choices for a long time.

Max didn't worry, though. He could tell that even as part of her relished the idea of having her apartment back to herself, another part of her did not want them to leave. Especially the boys.

He promised they would visit all the time. After all, they were only about a twenty minute drive away. On top of that, Mrs. Porter was still PB's main homeschooling teacher. But she refused to see it that way. Maybe a little distance would be a good thing. Her behavior towards Sandra had worsened, and the days of Little Max vanished. The latter another bonus to moving.

In his pocket, the brass key Lena Mobley had given him weighed him to one side. He planned to lock the thing in his desk drawer, but that would have to wait until he set up his desk. Or perhaps he would be better off taking it the Agency office. Anything involving a witch would be safer around a ghost detective instead of near a couple growing boys.

Drummond floated out of the roof and settled in front of them. "This is the last time I check through this house. There's nothing in the attic or foundation, nothing in the grounds, I don't see any signs of witchcraft, remnants of ghosts, or anything else that your darling wife wouldn't pick up on her own. If you want this house gone over anymore, you can call Irene. Psychics are good at this stuff, too."

"Thanks," Max said. He did appreciate Drummond giving the house a once over — well, a thrice over. Sandra could do it, of course, but she needed to help move in and focus on the boys. Plus, it gave Drummond a role to play. "Are you and Irene still an item?"

"It's not like that. I keep telling you."

"You know what they say about the guys who protest too much."

Drummond's mouth curled into a devilish grin. "You two enjoy your new home. Once your settled in, I'll be at our office waiting for you. And if I'm not there, you'll find me."

Sandra lifted her head from Max's shoulder. "You're going to see Irene right now, aren't you?"

"I'm a ghost of many talents. See y'all around." Drummond disappeared.

Sandra patted her hand against Max's chest. Her mother's ruby ring caught the sunlight as she looked at it.

J stepped out from behind them. Max startled. "Sorry there. I didn't see you. I thought you were inside the house."

J stared at the spot Drummond had been in. Then the boy lifted his head and watched PB carry another box inside. He turned around. "You two were just talking to a ghost, weren't you?"

Max looked at Sandra. He could feel the worry on his face. This was something they expected to have to deal with eventually, but at this point, Max would rather have had J ask about sex or drugs. However, he melted a little at the serene expression in his wife's eyes.

She said, "Yes, we were. He's our partner. His name is Drummond."

"So, ghosts are real?"

"Ghosts are real. And this is a big conversation we can have. Later."

J glanced back at the house. "Yeah. PB ain't ready to

hear any of this. But I think I am."

"We'll find some time. Promise."

J smiled as if he had just been promised a slice of ice cream cake. "Okay. I want to go look at my room now." He ran off.

Sandra gazed up at Max and they both burst into laughter. It flushed Max with warmth. Standing with his wife, with their feet firm on the ground, with their boys confident and safe — he closed his eyes and let it all fill him up. He had no doubt that the world would tilt once again, but for now, they would build this sturdy foundation. For now, they had each other and needed no more.

Afterword

Thank you for spending time with Max and the gang once again. It is greatly appreciated. Don't worry, I learned from Drummond not to get all mushy. Besides, you probably want me to get the good stuff right away. So, here it is:

As you might have guessed, much of the double murder case regarding Mary Goins is true. Wilburn Walker, John Smith, the shootout, and the unidentified man in the straw hat — all true. The case went to court as outlined, the transcripts were published in the press, and it all played out more or less as I described. Stranger still, the man claiming to be William Crutchfield did show up in California and did report to the police that he had killed people back in North Carolina at the time of the Goins murder. The departure from reality is after that moment. Crutchfield disappeared from the historical record, so I took all the liberties I wanted with his story from that point on. His involvement with witchcraft, witch hunting, and even coming back to North Carolina were all creations of my imagination. As was all indications that Mary Goins had anything to do with witchcraft.

While it is my fiction that Crutchfield not only came back to Winston-Salem but also contracted a disease on his trip, pest houses were a very real thing. There was a pest house located roughly where I placed the one in this story, and the photo I describe is real and of that particular house. However, the house is long gone. In fact, there are very few pest houses still in existence in the United States. They are, of course, no longer used but rather exist as historical sites for those who can find them.

Finally, if you ever come to Winston-Salem and put together your own Max Porter tour, do not try to find the Historical Society Building as I described it. It doesn't exist. There is a real building in Raleigh that handles all such matters, but the branch office in Winston-Salem was my own invention.

About the Author

Stuart Jaffe is the madman behind *The Max Porter Paranormal Mysteries,* the *Nathan K* thrillers, *The Parallel Society* series, *The Malja Chronicles, The Bluesman, Founders, Real Magic,* and so much more. His unique brand of old pulp adventure mixed with a contemporary sensibility brings out the best in a variety of SF/F sub-genres. He trained in martial arts for over a decade until a knee injury ended that practice. Now, he plays lead guitar in a local blues band, *The Bootleggers,* and enjoys life on a small farm in rural North Carolina. For those who continue to keep count, the animal list is as follows: one dog, two cats, two aquatic turtles, and fifteen chickens. The horse is now at a new pasture. She's having a wonderful time hanging with a herd of thirty other horses. Much better for her. As best as he's been able to manage, Stuart has made sure that the chickens do not live in the house.

DON'T MISS THE NEXT MAX PORTER!

OLD TRAGEDIES, NEW DANGERS

For Max and Sandra Porter, building a family seemed unattainable. But since moving to Winston-Salem and starting a business with the ghost of a 1940s detective, the unattainable did not sound so far-fetched. Over time, they brought two homeless boys into their work and eventually to their home.

But this *ad hoc* family has a lot of unknown histories. Dark secrets that threaten to crawl to the surface. When one of those secrets breaks through, Max finds himself in a fight -- not only for his own survival, but for the survival of his family as well.

If this family can't come together now, then they will be ripped apart forever.

It doesn't help that he has to worry about the Hull family and witches once more, but Max, Sandra, and Drummond have a lot on their side. Brains, magic, and the ghost world, too. Their enemies won't know what hit them.

Catch up with Max Porter!

From ancient curses to witch covens, World War II secrets to local lore, underground boxing to underground chambers, Max Porter and his team investigate it all.

Don't miss a single story in the bestselling series, the Max Porter Paranormal Mysteries.

And don't miss this unforgettable stand alone, time travel fantasy

REAL MAGIC

Duncan Rose, magician and card cheat, accidently slips back in time to 1934. Swindling his way through this new world, he searches for a doorway home, until a ruthless mobster takes notice - a man who wants to use time travel for his own purposes.

REAL MAGIC is an exciting time travel fantasy packed with real card tricks designed specifically for this story by renowned card magician, Cameron Francis.